Amanda —
I hope you
enjoy the
wild ride of
these women —
Thanks for all
you do —

REENU—YOU

Michele 2017

D1276177

MICHELE TRACY BERGER

This book is a work of fiction. The characters, incidents, and dialogue are drawn from the author's imagination and are not to be construed as real. Any resemblance to actual events or persons, living or dead, is entirely coincidental.

To Patricia Jane Brooks, who instilled in me the love of reading, the ability to laugh at myself, and incredible fashion sense. These gifts have served me well.

ONE

I always thought that I'd die somewhere in the Colorado mountains in a gruesome skiing accident. I'm a skilled skier but there is always an electrifying element of danger that makes the sport precarious as well as fun. My left knee might pop right out of the socket, severing delicate tendons, as it has done before when I try to do something too showy. And, after my knee popped out, I would fall back on the snow, injuring my body, breaking my lower back, hitting a tree at about seventy miles an hour. The pine trees with their prickly arms would embrace me and the slopes that I love would provide a picturesque burial site.

If I didn't die in the mountains, I surmised that I'd die somewhere at a posh ski club keeling over from a massive heart attack after I had outlived my usefulness as a ski instructor. At the very least, I hoped as everyone does, that I would leave this Earth wiser, a little thinner, moving right out of life's traffic into the path of something better. So far, none of my visions of death have come true.

A lot's been said about the early infected. I want to tell my story, because soon the virus will overtake me, too. The politicians, bureaucrats, and scientists shouldn't be the only ones who get to have their say about the virus and what it did. Despite its carnage, the virus did something special for me and for four other women.

I can remember the day that I went to buy Reenu-You. A shitty, humid New York morning greeted me in my mom's cramped apartment on Tremont Avenue in the Bronx. The Dominicans across the street had started their musical revelry consisting of Spanish reggae around eight a.m. Unless I'm skiing, I *never* get out of bed before eleven.

Coming from the store, my backpack was crammed with things that I needed for the next few days, my last ones in the city: fat-free cookies, unscented tampons, light bulbs, and six donuts from the Puerto Rican bakery around the corner. They were bowties, with thick white glazing running down the sides of the confection, pooling into the bag—the exact kind of food that I shouldn't have been eating. Like everyone else, I have a tendency to crave sweets when I'm stressed.

Though my mom and I were not extremely close, packing up her apartment after her death was the hardest thing that I ever had to do in my life, even though I had been through it once before with my father.

It was also so hard because I despise Nueva York. I'd lived in Queens and Brooklyn, was raised in the Bronx, although I hold all boroughs in equal contempt. I always feel hemmed in by the city, cut off from nature, like a cheating lover. Only my real lover is not made of ordinary bones and flesh; my paramour is fashioned from mountain peaks and snow that crunches underfoot.

My mom took me horseback riding, sometimes to the Catskills to compensate for living in urban dung. These respites as a child, however, were not frequent enough. Since she was an artist, she could see the beauty in just about anything, even eyesore crumbling brownstones. Even the way big fat water bugs skittered across the floor. Strange, I know.

Most importantly in the backpack sat the bottle of Reenu-You Relaxing Natural Miracle Hair Tonic (Reenu-You, for short). Rogaire (Ro, for short) had told me about it a few days after I arrived. I met pig-tailed Ro in the third grade and my only friend I knew from grade school who still lived in the city. When I came into the city on trips to see my mother, she got me current on the latest fashion tips, hairstyles, best places to eat, and where to go and be part of the hip crowd.

"Girl, Reenu-You makes your hair pretty, soft and straight. I know that you don't have anything like that in Aspen," Ro teased during our phone conversation a few days after my mom's funeral.

To be honest I was looking for a change, hairstyle just being one of the easiest and least complicated things to change about one's self.

After three years together, Peter and I had just broken up. With my mother recently dead, and I temporarily out of work from a major ski resort, what could I lose by trying a new hair product?

My hair is a dark chestnut brown, thick and worn in a clever bob processed with a variety of chemicals. I am always looking for new things to do with it because skiing dries out

9

my hair and makes it unnecessarily brittle. I don't care for braids, twists, dreads or other fancy African hairstyles as I already stood out on the slopes, and in Aspen.

"We're going to get you through this," Ro said.

I leaned into the warmth in her voice.

"You've gotten me through just about every hard thing. You probably need a break," I said.

"My life would've been boring all these years without you. You sure you don't want me to come and help? I can cancel the Atlanta trip," Ro said.

"No, I just want to get it over with. I'm almost done," I said. "Are you going to sign someone?"

"I'm checking out two groups, a female DJ and a boy band. Shouldn't take me long. I'll be back to see you off. Goodness knows I probably won't see you again unless I trek out to Aspen," Ro said.

"No, I'll come back for you. But Aspen's not so bad."

Ro made a small skeptical grunt. She had only been to Aspen once. I either traveled to see her and mom or we met somewhere in between. I wondered what life would be like without the anchor of my mom to connect me to New York. But, I thought, there still would be Ro.

"What are you doing with her bigger pieces?" Ro said.

"She arranged for Parsons to take most of her stuff," I said. "So efficient, she made it easy on me," I said feeling a tightening in my throat.

"I wish she would have told all of us sooner," Ro said with a slight dip in her effervescent voice.

"Yeah," I said. "People are the same in life and in death."

An uneasy silence passed between us before Ro continued, "Well, this hair tonic has been pumped on the radio and TV for the last month or so. It's blowing up! It's in a really funky female-shaped bottle. Unlike anything you've seen before."

"Oh? How much damage?" I said with interest.

"It's not so cheap, but get this—it's touted as a natural relaxer! No chemicals. Kat, it smells so good you could dip your fingers in and taste it. Reenu-You smells like honey and vanilla all mixed together."

"I like chocolate, myself," I said absentmindedly. We both laughed.

The rash, comprising small purplish discs with a green center, started around my hairline about two days later. I called Ro several times to see if she could refer me to any of her doctors but I couldn't get ahold of her. I didn't immediately make the connection about Reenu-You and the rash because my thoughts often returned to Peter, as if in a perpetual spin cycle. I missed Peter.

I thought hard about what Peter might be doing at any particular moment. He could be smiling at some woman, which he often did, showing off his gorgeous, all paid-for, middle-class teeth. Peter, my red-headed ex, who left me and the skiing world for dentistry. He said that I was living like a kid in a fantasy land (also known as Aspen) and he wanted to build a real life outside of skiing. I told him that fantasy is always better than reality and on his way out to give me back all my Everything but the Girl CDs. Thinking about him beat packing more of my mother's apartment, her artwork, her brushes, her pieces of charcoal. What was I supposed to do with her stuff?

Between thinking about Peter, my mother, and the rash, my mood plummeted. That's all I needed—to be stuck for another few days in the city while this breakout cleared up. I damn sure couldn't go back to Aspen and look for work like *this*. I stomped around the apartment periodically kicking packed boxes and the few pieces of furniture left. As this display of anger did not change my mood, I did about two dozen squats, which is always what I do when I'm in a deep funk. In my anxious and infectious state, I looked around the bathroom for something that would soothe my itching. The small gray and white garbage pail still overflowed with bottles of my mother's medications, but I found nothing useful there or under her tiny bathroom sink. Moving from room to room I searched out her purses, hoping to find something. From one, a tube of hydrocortisone and a small picture slipped out on to the rug.

The picture showed my family in Van Courtland Park. I was seven and remember the day well. My mom, as usual, looked gorgeous—a small brown woman with eyes that turned slightly up when she smiled due to the angle of her cheekbones, and wavy hair that flowed over her shoulders. She held my hand, and we were both looking up just as she had let go of my red balloons. My father had taken the picture. When I began to cry because she let my balloons go, my mother calmly said, "The wind wanted them." In the photo my eyebrows are raised and my hands outstretched.

A slow burn came over me as I stared at the photo. When was the last time that I wasn't so mad at her? Most of the time, everything about her made me mad. Her devotion to her art made me mad; her freedom made me mad. That she sent me to live with my dad's brother, Uncle Gene, in Vermont in my teens, rather than support me while she struggled as an artist made me mad.

I distracted myself by looking up some clinics in the area. I thought I probably just needed a stronger dose of hydrocortisone since I am a pretty hardy girl and am rarely sick. Skiing makes your body strong. In the phone book I found a clinic just four blocks away—probably crappy but all I needed was a little prescription-strength hydrocortisone, right? My stomach made grumbling noises and I decided on a quick lunch. I pulled a container of black bean soup from the refrigerator that a neighbor had delivered a few days ago, dumped it in a pot and heated it up.

My mother didn't own a television or computer, so I couldn't even channel-surf or get on AOL to see what I could find out. I sat and ate my soup, growing increasingly annoyed. Frustrated, I slammed down my empty bowl in the sink. I couldn't help but touch the bumps on my forehead. It was freaky because the rash felt familiar, like the quarter of an inch-long mole I have on my left leg, or the pebbled dark scar on my left hand that I got from a roller skating accident. Like it *belonged* there with all the other markings on my body. The rash was soft to the touch; it hadn't yet hardened into a crust. The discs, although ugly because of their mucous-green center, were arranged in a pattern of five. Five discs with a small green center. I'd never seen anything like this before. I felt my throat, my glands weren't sore and I wasn't running a fever. But, the rash itched, maddeningly. What the hell was this thing?

I foraged around the apartment again and opened a packed box full of my mother's hats, which I had intended on giving away. She loved them and accessorized them using her fanciful imagination. I eventually put on one of my mom's over-the-top straw hats with small vegetables twined together instead of the typical fruit. I felt silly with it on, but it was the only thing that covered my rash.

VOICEMAIL MESSAGE, PEOPLE'S CORNER

Brooklyn, July 1998

I'm leaving this message for Lorraine Simmons. Look around you. Look... Look, for God's sake! Folks are getting very sick. When you ask the doctors why, you get the fucking run around. They say, "It's a rash. Or, it's a skin condition, and it's nothing to worry about." Doctors working in that death trap of a hospital known as Carr Memorial don't know what it is. Some people go in and don't come back out. "Transferred," they tell us, but their families don't know where. A harmless skin rash, my ass. We're not seeing the whole picture. Since your organization is supposed to be doing something for this community I'd thought you'd damn well better know about it. Please investigate it. Please do something for us.

TWO

KAT

The clinic was in a building with a colorful mural along the side that read, "No violence in our neighborhood." Although faded in some places, I recognized the pictures of happy black and brown kids, and the elaborate flourishes with peace symbols on the guns. Mom's work.

After taking my ID the assistant looked at me with interest. Her nails were long, and painted white with red and black star decals near the nail beds. Having taken the forms I gave her, she looked me up and down and said, "Are you in any way related to Nicole Rodgers?

"Yeah, she was my mother," I said removing the straw hat, noting that it had lost some of its vegetables along the way.

"Oh, that is so cool, so cool. Hey, Jesus, come here," she yelled.

Jesus, a burly technician barreled out from the small office behind her.

"What? I'm not ready for the next patient."

"No, hon, it's not that, she. . . her mother, that's her daughter who did the mural thingy for the building. I recognized her name," she said, a triumphant smile crossing her face.

I shrugged my shoulders. I was used to this type of recognition all over the Bronx. Mom was always doing a mural here and there, usually giving away her art. That's why she never made money. "Oh baby, it's for a good cause," she'd say and wink at me. I inherited the bills, even in her death.

Looking around, I took note of the full house and bristled as I sat down on the gray plastic chairs. This looked it could take a while. The clinic was clean and covered with a plush gray carpet without any major spots or cigarette scorch marks, unlike some of the clinics that I had been to in the neighborhood as a child. The waiting room was filled with mostly women and children, as well as one Latino man, squeezed into a yellow formfitting dress. Back issues of magazines lay on the gray and white tables to my left—copies of *Centro* with a smiling blonde woman on the cover. People were reading the Latino newspaper, the *Diario,* and the latest *Essence.* We all sat in silence.

Sitting across from me, another black woman caught my eye. She had the exact same rash as mine on her face except that hers appeared spiral shaped, and it covered a good third of her forehead. Two skeins of golden yarn sat in her lap along with knitting needles that went untouched.

A bolt of fear flashed up from my stomach, just like when I take a wrong turn on the black diamond moguls. Was this rash contagious? Was *this* what I would look like in a few days—or worse, hours?

Her bleak gaze met mine and I quickly looked away. I stopped staring and tried to quiet my mind. For a few minutes, I listlessly flipped through the *Daily News*. The lead story was about a girl who had been raped by three men, thrown off a roof and left for dead. The *News* reminded me how much I hated New York.

Soon Jesus called a woman and her son, who vacated the seats next to the woman I had been watching earlier. Against my better judgment, I crossed the room to speak to her.

"Excuse me." I said. "I really hate to bother you."

The woman looked up as if from a trance, and I could see her square-shaped face clearly for the first time. Her rash looked terribly foreign, like it was swallowing her face with every turn of the spiral.

"You have it, too," I whispered.

"What? You mean this... this thing?" she said pointing to her face.

"You have it, too," I repeated, knowing it was rude but unable to look away.

"Does it hurt? Are you in pain?" Her rash *looked* painful, in addition to being more... developed than mine. The discs at the center of each spiral had hardened into overripe plum-colored crusts.

The woman shifted in her seat. "My brother said I should come, so I'm here."

I nodded, waited for more.

She leaned forward, beckoning me closer to her. "Mine talks to me," she added in a low voice.

I rolled my eyes and any concern I had been feeling for the woman evaporated. This is exactly why I hate New York—all the goddamn crazies. In Aspen, if you find people saying crazy things, they usually have a shitload of money and they are saying it to you at one of their lavish parties. You can stomach the crazy talk better because you're stuffing yourself with expensive food, free alcohol, and an almost endless supply of drugs. Either she was crazy, or she was playing crazy because she didn't want to be bothered. *Whatever.* Disgusted, I got up and took back my original seat across from her. She paid me no more mind and stared off into space, just like before.

As I waited, the number of patients in the room steadily increased—and several more women appeared with similar rashes on their faces. On some, the rashes almost looked like spores ready to pop. Before I knew it, it was already three o'clock. The receptionist clapped her hands and boomed an announcement. "Excuse me, everybody. I need your attention." She paused to clear her throat. "Dr. Serrano wants to know how many people have a rash on their face, back, or hands, and complaints of nausea."

Ten of us raised our hands.

"Okay, hold on. I'll be right back," she said with a false smile. She disappeared back into the farthest room.

She returned fifteen minutes later and spoke while waving those long nails around. "Okay, what we'd like everyone to do is to go to the Department of Health downtown. Dr. Serrano says—"

"Why can't we see Dr. Serrano?" I interrupted.

"He's talking to other doctors in the area," she snapped. Apparently, her enthusiasm for me as my mother's daughter was fizzling out.

"I have waited for over an hour," I continued. "Can you at least tell us what it is that we all have?"

"Ms. Rodgers, if I could do that, if *Dr. Serrano* could do that—he wouldn't have to refer you."

Jesus, came from behind, nodding, and added, "We've notified the Health Department. There are a few other patients with your... condition that have been referred there by some of the other Bronx clinics."

"Nothing serious I'm sure," the receptionist added, shuffling through papers.

"You're not sure of *anything*," I said.

As we departed, sucking his teeth, the drag queen quipped, "Tsk, tsk, y'all have been naughty girls-off to the officials."

"Shut up, Josephine. This one ain't funny." One of the women in the crowd shot back.

The Health Department? I wanted to walk around to think this over, but where could I go? A few coffee shops and a Wendy's populated the area near Yankee Stadium and 161st Street, but that would mean a brisk walk. I could take a subway downtown, but that option involved more people than I cared to see. I needed to deal with this thing soon. I wanted to leave this city ASAP.

"Where do we need to go?" I asked a woman wearing a faded Mets baseball cap and holding a squirming little girl.

"The Department of Health is on West 38th Street."

The other women around me grimaced and complained about the utter inconvenience of this nonsense. Our exodus would mean a trudge right through the middle of rush hour. I walked against the exiting women back to the receptionist.

"Yes, Ms. Rodgers?"

"Can you at least tell me who I need to see, or where I need to go when I get to the Department of Health?"

"The Contagious Diseases Department. All of you will need to see them," she said with lowered eyes.

Just then, I felt someone grip my shoulder. I swung around, coming face-to-face with the crazy woman from earlier. Her forehead jutted out with her prominent rash, giving a slight Neanderthal look to her face.

"What do you want?" I pulled away from her grip.

"Ask that it talk with you. It can. I've heard it." Her eyes were wide and serious.

"Leave me alone," I enunciated each word, low and clear.

I left the clinic, pushing through the crowd and once outside whistled at the first gypsy cab I saw.

THREE

CONSTANCIA
August 1998, The Bronx

The bottle, yo, I don't even know how to say it. On the counter, right? When I picked it up, the bottle was just glowing in my hand. It felt warm and shit. I couldn't take my hand off of it. Yeah, check it out.

"Are you playing with the bottle, or are you going to buy it?" This bug-eyed Asian girl, with overdone green eye shadow, screamed out at me from behind the cash register and broke my concentration.

"Shut the fuck up, puta. I'm checkin' it out, okay?"

I come here all the time to this rinky-dink store, with dusty merchandise, and all I can get is crap like that. That's why I want to live out in the burbs, in Connecticut, like my rich cousins. The cashiers know where it's *at* in those stores. No one gets edgy when you're just looking to buy something, they treat you well. Not like this stupid little bitch. It's the little things about living in the ghetto that really piss me off. Anyway, I should have known the way that bottle seemed to glow in my hand that *something* was up. The bottle felt too good, but I was drawn to it.

I fingered the bottle again. People had been telling me about this Reenu-You stuff. Check it out: the bottle was hype. I had never seen a hair relaxer that came in a fancy maroon bottle shaped like a curvy woman. The bottle shape reminded me of some of the mamis that strut proud on 149th street. The bottle's shape is not like me at all though—I'm a rail, if that. A stickbug. But hey, I can fit into clothes that women would give their Weight Watchers coupons for.

But this was different, eh? Reenu-You cost twice as much as what other relaxers like Lustersilk and Dark and Lovely cost.

The warmth of the bottle made me feel good. *Yes*, I thought, *hell yes*, this product is going to hook my head *up*. There was something about the bottle that made me happy. I placed both my hands around it, slipping it in my basket along with some gum for me and foot powder for my brother. It was expensive, but I deserved it. After all, in just another month I'd start taking my first set of classes for my Associates Degree in accessory design at the Fashion Institute of Technology! Oh my God, all my scrimping and saving and studying… it was all finally paying off. I was born knowing how a good shoe or purse could rock an outfit. The fall most definitely was going to bring some big changes to my life. Clothes always help me express myself, the way that I want to be in the world. I've already planned out my entire wardrobe for school. My hair is the last thing I need to take care of to look the part of an up and coming student designer!

I'm Puerto Rican and I have a head full of nappy hair. But I do something about it, you know? The sisters around the way like Angelica and Janey see me and compliment me on my hair all the time. They think that my hair is naturally straight. My mom used to say: "Puerto Ricans are first-class cousins to niggers. So what can you expect when it comes to hair?"

Straightening my hair is mandatory. Hector, my boyfriend, likes it and every female in my family relaxes their hair like serious clockwork. Well, it's because the guys like it. They don't want no girl with short, kinky hair. You know how it is.

No one can talk to me against my Hector. He's a bit rough around the edges, but he's fun and we always go out dancing. Salsa, house, reggae, whatever I want. He's also happy that I don't have any kids. No kiddos for me now. I don't have time for getting caught up in the mommy life. I'm not going to make that mistake—like so many girls in my neighborhood do. They want to create something good and so do I, but I want to get paid for it and have what I create become a household name.

Later on I went back to my place and used Reenu-You. Whenever I do my hair, I think of my best friend of a long time ago, Robin, three years older than me. Robin used to do my hair until she moved away. She was the only sister who ever knew I straightened my hair. It's just not something you tell, it's something you *do*. She was a little yellow thing, freckly, and she always wore a white headband. Being with her was so cool until she moved away. My mom even liked her, probably because Robin didn't look like the typical black girls around the way. I learned so much from her like how to braid hair, how to apply makeup, and how to pluck my eyebrows. That's how girls learn about how to be beautiful—from each other.

I called Hector and asked him to come over, then sat down with some yellow rice full of sausage (it's the one dish that I can eat anytime), and waited for Reenu-You to work its magic. From the moment it touched my head I knew this was some powerful shit. That warmth that I felt in the store now flooded my whole body. It felt like your mother tucking you in and giving you a kiss—your body's just happy to be alive. The product itself was surprisingly gooey; way too gooey for a regular hair relaxer. After a few minutes longer on my head, the warm mother-tucking-you-in feeling disappeared and was replaced with tingling at the nape of my neck, like a relaxer that's left on too long. You know, when the tingling feeling turns to feeling like someone is using your head as a pincushion. I had this strange feeling, like that white goo was sinking into me, going through my dark, kinky hair into my scalp, hunting for the core of me. I swear that's what I thought. *It's becoming a part of me.*

But I didn't wash it out until the time was up.

As soon as I finished puking my brains out later that night. I knew that something was wrong. When I saw the bumps, all over my head, neck, and face, I cried. I didn't even want to go downtown to do the remaining paperwork for my first semester at FIT.

Hector got close, bringing a black lamp, from an end table, over and shining it right on my head.

"It's ugly, that's for sure," he said.

"You ain't telling me nothing that I don't already know," I snapped. Hector could be very blunt, that was his way, but today I really didn't appreciate it.

My brother knocked on the door, "Constancia, I got back from Rockbottom's."

He opened the door "Here, I got this. . ." his voice trailed off. He held out a paper bag.

"Oh, gracias, gracias." I snatched the bottle from the paper bag, and pulled it out, not paying attention to anything he said. "This will make me feel better."

Watching me walk over to the bathroom, Hector said, "Your head might be fucked up, but you still got a nice ass."

I turned and smiled, "Thanks for thinking about the important things in life, Papi."

He shrugged, and sat on my bed playing with my Snoopy pillow. "I call it as I see it... Yeah, Naomi Campbell got nothing on you except that she's black and famous."

"This is serious, Hector. What if I'm scarred from these bumps?"

"Oh, relax. It's probably some kind of chemical reaction."

Ignoring him, I ripped open the bottle and poured the liquid to the cotton balls I had left out on the makeup counter, frantically dabbing at my face and neck. A burning sensation came over me so suddenly that tears sprang from both my eyes, and I screamed. "Shit! It's burning. . . Oh Jesus, cabron!" My whole head felt like it was on fire.

"Jesus Christ, what is it?" Hector came running over.

"Witch Hazel is supposed to soothe." I choked out, and then actually looked at the plastic bottle in my hands for the first time. "100% Rubbing Alcohol."

My face stinging with red-hot pain, I stormed out to the living room where my good-for-nothing brother was watching the *Price is Right*.

"You idiot! You complete imbecile! You lazy ass! You didn't even read the label! This almost burnt my skin off! I told you to get witch hazel, not rubbing alcohol!"

"What?" he took his headphones off.

My hands shook and I could feel myself spiraling into a fit. It's like when I watched that weather program about a tornado. First, you see just a flat boring field and nothing for miles, and then all of a sudden a giant twister comes barreling out of nowhere. That's me. I ripped the headphones out of the television and threw them against the wall. *No one* ever did anything around this house right except me.

"Why don't you calm the fuck down?" Hector shouted from the bedroom.

My stupid-ass brother got alcohol instead of witch hazel and it burned me so bad I couldn't speak. It was like the rash was moving into my skin to get away from it. Imagine that, a smart-ass rash. "Who are you telling to calm down?" I yelled back.

Hector came in the living room and said, "Look, stop being a puta! Get your head together."

"How was I supposed to know? Witch hazel. Rubbing alcohol. It's like the same thing!" my brother whined.

"Yeah, stop being so hard on him," Hector said.

I turned the full force of my tornado toward Hector, jabbing him in the chest with my finger. "If you are going to insult me, Hector, then you can leave." My face was still on fire.

Hector got real quiet. Then nodding he said, "That's it. Look, you call me when you get your fucking head and face together. All you care about anyway is your fucking looks!" He left and slammed the door.

I couldn't believe that he would say that to me after all we had been through. Jesus! He was being a prick. What about the time that he couldn't fuck for a month because he was stressed out about getting a job? Did I take it out on him by sleeping with someone else, or God forbid, saying something about his manhood?

"You're damn right I care about my looks!" I screamed.

I threw the bottle of alcohol at the front door.

"You're a little bitch," my brother said.

"Shut up! My head hurts and my face is all messed up, no thanks to you. I'm going to the clinic."

As I pulled on some jeans I thought maybe I was being punished like my mother always said I was going to be for not living a strict Catholic life, or for being a girl. Those were the two bad things that I had going against me. Ma always said, "Hermanas, they make you poor. They always need dresses, gifts, and sweet things."

I couldn't go out into the street looking like this, with my hair, and my rash, and, oh Jesus, my face. I grabbed my brother's Yankees cap—finally, he was good for *something* today. A whole chunk of my hair fell out as soon as the hat touched my scalp. I looked in horror at the chunk of hair on the ground, the little globby bits of hair follicles were swollen white masses at the end of the hairs. I wanted to yell at the top of my lungs. Where was my Hector and his big strong arms? Oh my God, Hector, *Hector*? Why did I chase him away?

"On the way back from Dr. Serrano's—that's who you're going to, right? Can you get some Bud? I'm all out and Jose Rod and Milagros are coming over tonight." My brother was standing in the doorway to my room.

"My fucking hair is falling out—fuck you!" I ran past him and out the front door.

On the way to the clinic I thought about the different sorry-ass men in my life. My brother, a thirty-six-year-old waste who constantly milked some combined form of unemployment and welfare. My father worked all the time so he wasn't ever there. And Hector, surely he couldn't have meant what he said. He loved the way I looked.

I touched my face. A piece of advice mother gave to me before she died when I was twelve, six years ago, came back to me. "You're not blanca like your cousins, but use your face to the best advantage." That was what I was trying to do with Hector—I needed my face. In another two years I wanted him to marry me. I'd have my degree in accessories and everything would be good, for a change. He was just bugging out, that's all.

In the midst of all this fantasizing as I was walking downtown, I noticed that something was... off. My body felt so strange. I started breathing in and out real quick. I put my nose next to a big-ass wire garbage can and nothing. *Nothing.* I was walking one of my favorite streets in the neighborhood, and I couldn't smell the Cucifritos place with roast pork and rice and beans piled up high in the window. I couldn't smell the soul food Chinese place that sold the fried chicken wings, soaked in unnaturally red colored hot sauce, and musky fried rice. I stopped short with my nostrils flaring, and I almost bumped into a short, black girl with a beige leather bag in her hand. I couldn't smell the jasmine oil that I had put on after my shower that morning. I couldn't smell a damn thing.

Shit.

INTERNAL VIDEO PRESENTATION, KRYSTÀLAVOX CORPORATION

Chicago, July 1997

Dana Cooper, CEO

We have discovered the mix of botanicals that will solve one of the great dilemmas for women who desire perfect, smooth, straight hair. And this is how we are going to sell it: by saying it's so good, so natural, and so safe, that you could eat it if you wanted to. Good, natural, and safe. These aren't artificial words, or just a catchy sales hook.

I'd like you each to pick up the bowl next to you and smell it. Smells great, right? Now, please dip your finger into it. And now, taste it. Yes, go ahead! Delicious, right? There is truth in this advertising.

I've already mentioned the rise of botanical marketing within the hair and skin industry. We project that potential revenue in botanicals will outpace every other sector of the beauty industry over the next four quarters. Thanks to our internal research, we know that our competitors' product lines, like Great Tresses' Gentle Relaxation, for example, or World of Hair's Au Natural, currently use a combination of lavender, myrrh, aloe, arnica, orris, and balm mint as primary ingredients for their proprietary formulas. The Recognizing African Beauty line tripled their holdings last year when they introduced a "natural" line of hair products.

The idea of gentle, natural hair treatments is gaining in popularity. Over the last two months, Hair Today has run five articles on the topic, and plans on devoting a regular monthly column to natural hair care tips and product recommendations. Even if the science behind the natural trend is inconclusive and under-researched, consumers don't seem to care.

We are presented with a unique opportunity here, to seize the market just as the natural botanical trend is primed to explode. Our competitors' products are not only of lower quality, but they have also failed to launch integrated marketing and advertising campaigns that emphasize this burgeoning trend. They have not tapped into an increasingly health conscious group of minority women consumers—Heart and Soul magazine, and the corresponding television show, are just one cultural litmus test showing just how mainstream "natural" can be.

And now, ladies and gentlemen of the board, I would like to introduce you to the product of the future.

Presenting Reenu-You Relaxing Natural Miracle Hair Tonic! It is the first all-natural chemical-free relaxer. Everything about this product will be original, in its proprietary formula, in its design, and in its cutting-edge marketing plans. We'll market through the stylist community first, of course along, with direct marketing, infomercials and radio. We'll begin in Chicago and New York, immediately.

We are going to put traditional relaxers out of business and make a fortune.

FOUR

KAT

Complete pandemonium at the Department of Health reigned when I arrived. Women with bright green snot-faced children dashed past me, drug addicts nodded off in the hallway, and yet others with tell-tale rashes just like mine all made their way through the long lobby. There was no one directing the flow of traffic. *What exactly does the Department of Health do,* I wondered? From a black steel desk, a man with dreadlocks and sunglasses resting on his forehead asked, "Do you need an HIV test?"

I frowned. "Not that I know of. Can you tell me where I might find Contagious Diseases?" I asked.

Openly gawking at my forehead he mumbled, "Oh yeah, you want to take those steps over there on the left and get on the orange elevator, it will take you up to the eighth floor."

"Thanks."

"You should… when you finish, of course, come back for an HIV test. Everyone needs one."

"Whatever." I said. I took off my ridiculous hat and stepped on the elevator.

Stepping off the elevator, if I hadn't seen it with my own eyes I would have thought I was dreaming or making it up. Every chair in the waiting area had a woman or child in it. Women slouched against the walls. I recognized a few faces from the first clinic. Other than those familiar faces all the other women were of brown and black hues similarly marked with the same spiral pattern on their arms, necks, and around the eyes. We looked a sight with our splotched faces and necks.

I tensed up and gritted my teeth. Living in Aspen for the past six years, I guess I felt exposed in this bustling area. Straight up, I am a loner. Most skiers are. The real skiers, that is, who are focused on their craft, not perpetually drugged out or sleeping with everyone. As I walked around trying to find out where to sign in I felt the women's eyes on me. I felt as if those women could read me, categorizing me: the nonurban one, the different one. The one dressed in khaki shorts, Tevas, with an old Pat Benetar T-shirt on. The one not from the city. As Ro would say, I didn't have a "city flava" to me at all.

I avoided the crazy woman from the clinic who glared at me as I approached the front desk. She turned her attention to whatever she was knitting that lay in her lap. The receptionist, a freckled, badly-aging blonde, handed me a stack of forms, "Find a seat where and when you can," and looked back down at her mound of paperwork.

After filling out the forms I quickly went to the bathroom to check on the progress of my rash. It had grown considerably, now covering my ears and neck. I gripped the bathroom sink. I looked freakish. Someone had better have some answers for me when I get to see a doctor! *If* I got to see a doctor.

It was like déjà vu from the clinic: we sat and waited. The doctors bustled back and forth from one end of the hallway to the other. After an hour they moved us to another waiting area where there had to be at least thirty more women with the same tell-tale rash.

"Who are you people anyway? Where are the doctors?" These questions spoken so loudly and confidently caught my attention. I had started to doze. A wicker-colored brown woman with a pink and black scarf wrapped around her head, stockings rolled down around her ankles, stood and shook her fists over the receptionist's counter. Something moved near her. It was an old dog curled in a ball, one so unbelievably fat that when it unrolled herself and stood, her nipples almost hit the floor. The dog's legs receded so far into her body that it didn't look like it could walk very well. I noticed with interest the color of the dog's fur—an animal cracker tan. The dog's color was unreal, just as unreal as the fact that the owner *had* a dog at the Department of Public Health.

"I am Pearlie and this," she gestured at the enormously fat, beige dog, "is Peggy." The pursy woman announced to everyone and no one in particular, "And like the rest of you I want to know what the hell is going on. Haven't we answered enough questions and filled out enough forms?"

"One woman said, "¡Sí, tenemos que hablar con un médico YA MISMO!" Others feigned sleep or said under their breath, "Esta mujer está loca."

"Some of us have been here for three hours."

"Yes," another woman chimed in.

Pearlie looked around the room nodding her head. An attendant came toward her with a sour look on his face, "Ma'am, you can't have any animals here. This is an area for infectious people. We need to keep this area as free of germs as possible."

"Oh, I can just about *die* from waiting but you want to take my dog. Don't you come near my dog! I couldn't leave her at home."

The dog instinctively knew its cue and half ran and half rolled away, dragging its ass from Pearlie and the attendant. Pearlie tried to follow and then stopping for a moment she held herself. Peggy ran a little farther and stopped. And then came an awful hiccupping and gurgling sound, and Pearlie kneeled down and vomited. This got everyone in motion. Everyone jumped up to help. Attendants and nurses left their stations and one doctor at the end of the hall bolted toward her. Within a few moments they got her to her feet, escorting her away from the two small puddles she made.

I yelled over to the dog while many attended to the woman.

"Pearlie... Peggy." Shit, I couldn't remember the dog's name.

"Stop it! Whatever your name is," I shouted as the dog licked up her mistress's puke.

They moved us to yet another sterile, boring room. This room had no artwork in it, no color, cramped and with two-year-old magazines. We could all just die right here, I thought.

Being raised by an artist I tend to look at rooms differently than most people. I ask, where's the color? Or, the variance and texture? Maybe that's why my mother chose to forego surgery. A bland hospital room would have sent her right over the edge. She didn't tell anybody that she was dying of breast cancer. By the time she did, it was too late. I barely got a chance to say an awkward good-bye to her.

"Your life is your art," she told me when I was young. I had no idea what she meant then. Don't know if I know what it means now.

The light brown-skinned girl, sitting next to me, broke my concentration when she addressed the whole room. "My name is Constancia, and I'm bored as hell."

She smacked her gum wide and hard through a set of strong white teeth. My neck started to tingle as it always does when I can't stand someone. This Constancia looked all of twelve, just ridiculous in the blue baseball cap, the too-tight and too-short red bolero jacket that accentuated her small waist and pointed breasts. Stiletto boots capped her jeans. Her eyes were blessed with long eyelashes, a complexion like wheat bread dunked in weak tea. Although bone thin and tall, nothing seemed frail about her; I sensed a ferocity to her. She made the room smell of bubble gum and jasmine oil.

"You know what's making us all sick, don't you?" *Smack, smack... smack smack.*

"I'd give you all the money in my purse if you really knew because I have an important event to go to later tonight and I can't show up like this," a woman with hazel eyes and a pouty mouth said, holding up purplish rash-infected hands.

There were amens and uh-huhs from several of the other women.

"Did any of you use a thing called Reenu-You? It's a hair tonic? I knew it when I put that crap on my head. It felt strange," Constancia said pulling on her red bolero jacket.

"Nah, that ain't it. I used that almost two weeks ago," a woman with short wavy platinum colored hair said, shaking her head.

"I don't want to believe it. I've never had any problems with a hair relaxer. Don't jump to conclusions," another woman said, pointing to Constancia.

"I'm not," Constancia replied, "I'm adding up two plus two. Something's wrong with that product."

Another woman sat up and pulled off a floppy beach hat exposing clumps of hair colored in a shocking emerald green and brown patchwork, and a large oozing sore above her left eyebrow. "She might be right," she said pointing to Constancia, "because my hair turned green and this rash ain't normal!"

Though a few women continued to debate with Constancia, most of us were quiet, reflecting on when and where we had used Reenu-You. Despite these naysayers, many women nodded in stubborn agreement.

"God, I was just fine before I decided to try that purple bottle. Why did I ever take a chance with a new product?" a tall woman wearing a short beige skirt and a blue cutoff top said.

"My stylist recommended it and she has never steered me wrong," the woman wearing the beach hat said.

Someone else said, "That damn commercial was on all the time and it was so seductive!"

Many women nodded their heads.

Pearlie who seemed recovered from her vomiting fit, was wrapped in a blanket, holding a cup of water. "The girl is on to something, somebody get the doctor."

Several of us scrambled up to do so.

From: Lynx Dupree
To: Dalton Rutland, Director of Operations, KrystàlaVox
Corporation
Subject: Product #1165
Date: April 20, 1997

Dear Dalton,

I wanted to clarify some points that I made during our meeting.

First, I know that it has been a rocky path since Krystàla-Vox's transition and I know I am still adjusting. I am grateful that I'm able to stay on with the company that my mother built.

Second, I am also enthused about my potential formula for product #1165. I do want to caution your excitement, however, about the timeline to market. Since you have cut the research and development wing of the company, I am finding it is taking longer to do a thorough testing of the formula. No one else you've brought in from KrystàlaVox's has ever worked in hair care product development. So, it is taking me a longer time to conduct the basic research and do it in a comprehensive way. I don't think product #1165 will be ready to market for at least another year.

Sincerely,

Lynx Dupree

Lynx Dupree
Senior Research Consultant

FIVE

KAT

Three doctors, two women and a man came back and looked impatient with us for bothering them. The man introduced himself as the supervising doctor for the unit. When we explained what the possible connection was they were quiet for a minute. The male doctor turned to a younger, freckled, brunette female doctor and in a stentorian voice said, "You mean you didn't ask them if they had put something unusual on their scalp?"

"I thought that it was a... It just didn't occur to me." She sighed tilting her head to the side, her face thin and unadorned.

They took down the name of the product and seemed mildly disappointed that we didn't have it in our possession. Did we have to do their job for them?

"Maybe it's some kind of chemical reaction... you know?" I offered.

"Yes, hair relaxers have lye in them—that's their base, even the so called no-lye-relaxers have got lye in them, I don't care what the manufacturers say," said a lithe woman who had been quiet during our earlier conversation, her skin a shade darker than honey with two braids tucked behind her head. Her hands were deeply affected by the rash, but there was just one small spiral over her right eye.

"Yeah, 'hair tonic.' What a joke," the woman with green hair said.

The doctors nodded sympathetically. The older female doctor said, "From the tests that we have done, we don't think the rash is chemically based, but we'll check this tip out."

In listening to them I realized they no real idea what a hair relaxer really was or what it did. I felt myself becoming invisible to them. We all were becoming invisible to them. It was as if they were looking right through all of us.

As the time dragged on, the doctors started to call each one of us in for examination, then back out to the waiting room. They took blood again and urine samples.

Later, the same three physicians walked back in the room. The head doctor said, "There isn't a whole lot of good news, I'm afraid."

"That's the story of my life," someone said in a loud voice.

"We think it's a virus, and it is a type of virus that acts very differently than most." He paused and surveyed the room. "A traditional virus, as you may know, gets into your cells and changes them, imprinting them with different signals."

"Spare us the bio lesson and just get to the point, doc," the gum-chewing rail-thin young woman said.

"I actually would like to hear the 'bio lesson' if you don't mind," I said loudly, shooting her a glare. Who was this kid anyway?

Ignoring the both of us, the young female doctor cleared her throat. "What we don't understand is why it is reproducing itself so quickly, how it is transmitted, and which receptors it has bonded to."

"Receptors are the key links to understanding viruses." the mature female doctor offered. When she spoke, her heavy cheeks puffed out, reminding me of a chipmunk.

"While we haven't had time yet to discover how it affects you, we have some good clues to go on. We can examine your symptoms and determine which systems in the body are being affected. For example, Ms. Jorge can't smell a thing," she continued. The annoying young woman, Constancia, nodded.

The younger brunette doctor picked up the thread and continued to explain. "Some of you have experienced constant vomiting, while others have bad headaches. Preliminary tests and examination results suggest that the two main systems being affected are the olfactory system and the gastrointestinal system—"

"What about the way we look—our skin," Pearlie interrupted.

"Yes, yes well that's just a cosmetic side effect, unpleasant for sure, but in and of itself, appears inconsequential," she said with a wave of her hand.

I sucked air through my teeth. *Inconsequential?* Sure, doc.

"Am I the only one that can hear what this thing is thinking?" the crazy woman, with yarn and knitting needles in her lap, piped up for the first time since I'd seen her earlier that day.

"Are you hearing voices?' The male doctor asked, his expression vaguely surprised.

"That's a whole other kind of problem," a woman with a gap between her teeth quipped, her rash had spread all over the front of her face and down her chest.

"I'm not hearing voices. I'm hearing what's inside of me, of us. It's a part of us now, there's nothing you can do."

Other women gave her a strange look and shook their heads, even physically backing away from her.

A brief smile crossed the male doctor's face, as if such a dire outlook amused him. "Well, let's not take a fatalistic view... Mrs. Parker, is it?"

He continued, "There are many viruses in the world, and this one is sure to match up with one that we have seen before. The only problem would be if it is mutating into a different *type* of virus, but most known viruses don't do that quickly. Our virologist isn't here, so we're little understaffed today."

"A mutating virus! That's serious," a woman said.

"What about Reenu-You?" Constancia asked.

"Yeah," Pearlie said nodding, clapping.

He shook his head. "We're ruling that out. Viruses just don't come from hair products." The other doctors nodded.

"A hair relaxer would be a very strange source for a virus," the young female doctor said.

"This city is full of strange shit happening," Pearlie added.

I could feel the heat and frustration of the day take its toll. We were not going be nice, quiet and compliant. The room erupted in questions, comments and even shouts.

"Listen to that girl!"

"I was feeling fine before putting that stuff on my head!"

The male doctor held out his arms, waving them slightly trying to placate the crowd of angry brown women. "But, uh we're still checking out all leads. But there's not biologically active agents in over the counter...."

The older female doctor leaned forward and said, "There is a difference between causation and correlation. Just because many of you used this product doesn't mean it caused your symptoms. They may seem rel–"

"You're supposed to be helping us, not talking down to us. We're not stupid," Pearlie interrupted.

"What are you not telling us?" The gap-toothed woman interjected, glaring at them.

The doctors looked at each other for a moment before the male doctor resumed his annoying, placating tone. "Please, ladies, please calm down. There is nothing to be alarmed by. We understand this news is unexpected and is terribly inconvenient."

"You damn right, it is!" the gap-toothed woman stood up angrily, fists clenched.

Their answers weren't satisfying to me at all. In fact, the longer they tried to spin, the more unconvincing and uninformed they sounded.

The young doctor looked around at the room, the first glimmers of panic showing in her eyes. "This is a very low level contagion situation. The CDC representatives—that is, the Centers for Disease Control officers—are flying here tonight. They will investigate the epidemic."

"What CDC? What epidemic?" I felt like that kid in that ridiculous sitcom of the 1980s *Different Strokes*, "What are you talking about, Willis?"

"You see…" the eldest female doctor began, excruciatingly articulating every syllable, as if we didn't have an unidentified virus infecting us, but were recovering patients from a routine lobotomy, "An *epidemic*, according to the medical community's definition, occurs when three people come into see us, or any doctor, and are diagnosed with either a known or unknown disease or viral infection." She smiled and widened her eyes at the last, like a storyteller reaching the end of a fairytale.

"The staff will make you comfortable here while you wait," she concluded, then strode away murmuring to her colleagues, discussing how many "microns" this virus was and other things that we peons could not understand.

REENU-YOU COMMERCIAL, DEMO ONE OF FIVE:

May 1997

EXT. A BEACH

Soft, non-distinct "tropical" music plays in the background. The camera pans across a tropical beach with blue skies, then cuts to a variety of dark and light-skinned models walking toward the camera. The words REENU-YOU appear at the bottom of the screen.

An African American young woman plunges her finger in a ceramic bowl, cream colored goo sticks to her fingertip. She suggestively licks the goo off her finger.

The screen flashes with the message, "It even tastes good!"

A split-screen video of the same African American model appears side by side. In the left-hand screen, her hair is frizzy and uncombed, and she grimaces at the camera. In the right-hand frame, Reenu-You is coating the model's hair. The model with Reenu-You smiles.

The images split away to reveal the same model flipping a curtain of straight and well-styled hair over her shoulder.

> MALE VOICE
>
> That's right, folks. Now this is a real alternative to hair relaxers. It's a hair tonic. Just like the name implies— this is a product that improves hair. This is a no-lye relaxer, and that's why we call it a hair tonic. And, that's no lie. This product comes to you from where?

> MODELS
>
> Brazil, Guyana, and Malaysia.

MALE VOICE

This product contains the most
amazing mix of plants from all
over Mother Nature's garden.

The camera cuts to a brown hand with man-
icured pink nails sweeping away bottles
and kits of well-known hair relaxers.

MALE VOICE

You won't have to throw away
any more of your hard earned
money on messy and expensive
products.

MODELS

Join the Reenu-You revolution!

SIX

KAT

"Ah, I am so restless. Waiting and waiting. I feel like a fucking lab rat. We should get out of here." As Constancia paced the room, she popped her gum more aggressively, louder. Another two hours had passed and *still* nobody had come for us.

Five of us sat together now. Pearlie went around asking our names. The crazy woman's first name was Doris. She had a Macy's bag full of different yarns, a purple ball now out, being knitted into something. The other two women left in the room were Constancia, the crude gum snapper, and Sandra, the tall, willowy woman with the plaits, who exuded grace and elegance, but who hadn't spoken much. The other patients from earlier had dispersed to make phone calls to anxious husbands, fathers, lovers, and sisters. To someone. I had no one to call.

I noticed as the room emptied that I could breathe a bit easier. I felt slightly more comfortable now, less claustrophobic. We each looked around at the five of us left in in the room with interest. I felt the subtle release of my breath. Something in the air shifted. I couldn't put my finger on it but I noticed I felt more relaxed with the fewer number of women in the room.

Pearlie broke our silence. "Me and Peggy know somewhere to go. We, all of us, need to go away from here and think together for a little while."

Now why would we want to go anywhere with you? I thought.

"Yes. It's been such a long day, it would be nice to get away from this building for a bit," Sandra said with a stretch. She had a broad flat nose and lips so full, the edges seemed to curl up into a smile by themselves regardless of her intention.

"I don't want to go back to my house right now," Constancia said. *Pop, pop, smack.* She was working that gum, and it was working my nerves.

"Have you noticed how less fidgety we are when it is just us?" Doris asked.

I just had it about up to my eyeballs with her. "I'm going to get a soda or something... if the doctors ever come back, let them know, I'm down the hall." I said moving across the room.

We hadn't seen hide nor hair of any of the doctors for at least an hour. *What the fuck?*

"Wait sister, slow down. Listen to me. We need to be together, the five of us." Doris put her knitting down.

I rolled my eyes, ready to retort when Pearlie cut into the tension. "Well, girls, before I left, I had a pot of greens on the stove that wouldn't be nothing to heat up, and some chicken spiced up real good, all ready to go into the oven. I also got some peach pie, which was a pain in the ass to bake in this heat, mind you. I also got some soda that you don't have to pay an outrageous price for," she said winking at me. "It's just me and Peggy, so wouldn't be no trouble at all. Coming to my house that is."

I could feel my stomach agree it had been a long day with little food. And certainly no really good food. Plus, I never got much "down home" food growing up because my mom was a terrible cook. She almost set the apartment on fire cooking stuffed green peppers.

"The doctors probably aren't going to have any real answers today. It's Friday, you know," Sandra said with a fluid shrug.

Doris said, "Best offer I've had all day," and started to put away her knitting.

"I'm staying. I'm... trying to wrap some things up. I'm leaving the city soon," I stammered.

"Oh, I see," Pearlie said and gave me a look like she expected more of me before dropping her gaze.

Inside my gut it felt like a cord had been cut, but I ignored it. I am expert at ignoring things I don't understand. My mother in particular, relationships in general.

I walked away from the women and looked for a vending machine, digging into my shorts for some change. After finding myself lost in a maze of hallways, I stopped and leaned against a wall, heavy with the weight of memories. I sagged to the floor. I thought about home, more boxes, and more of my mom's art. I remembered Ro was out of town and wouldn't be back until late tonight. I pictured myself alone in that horrible apartment, with a bottle of wine, reliving my crushing breakup with Peter, of my last days with my mother, watching her disappear in front of my eyes. I just couldn't do it. I thought about Pearlie's invitation. An older city person doing something nice for younger folks, how often did that happen? Like, *never*.

I leapt up, followed the exit signs and ran down flight after flight of steps, hoping I could still catch them before they left. Thank God for my knees, my squats, my butt, my ability to move. I kept telling myself I could come back here if I didn't like her place. I didn't see any staff as I tore through the hallways. The ground floor was completely deserted, a dead zone. Where was everyone? The posted hours said they were open until 6:30, and it was only 6:00.

I caught the women just as they were heading out the main door. Pearlie winked at me, waving me along to join them.

"So now the question is how do we all get to this old lady's apartment?" Constancia pulled her baseball cap lower, trying to shield her face from view.

"We could just take a taxi to where you live," I said to Pearlie.

"An excellent idea, Kat. I'm so glad you changed your mind," Pearlie said.

The sky darkened and the first few raindrops fell as we got to the curb.

Sandra, the graceful woman with the full lips, looked the most normal so we let her hail a cab. She stepped forward with perfect posture and a dignified air about and easily summoned a cab. We all piled in. Peggy flattened herself underneath our feet, let out a whimper, and Pearlie roared, "The Bronx, 180th Street and the Grand Concourse. Pronto, we're sick women."

The cab stopped in front of a building that used to be nice. You could close your eyes and almost picture when the large ornate front gate gleamed white and the trees planted in the square in the middle filled out during spring. If you stood there long enough, you could imagine hearing families talking and laughing, in Yiddish, German, Polish, and Italian.

But in reality, the gate itself had graffiti sprayed on it and the lock had been broken. Anemic shrubs huddled together in the corners of the square. And the sounds ranged from the fight on the fifth floor between a man and his woman to the five o' clock news blaring from a window. Still, climbing the steps to Pearlie's apartment I marveled at the building's internal up keeping—the hallways were clean, with beautiful, decorative glass windows still intact, and weighty doors separating each floor from the world outside.

Finally, we reached Pearlie's floor. Flinging open the front door of her apartment Pearlie said, "Have a seat anywhere you can find one." We entered a large living room cluttered with stacks of yellowed paper clippings, and boxes everywhere.

Pop. Pop. Smack. Phew. Constancia's gum must be losing its elasticity by now.

"You've got a lot of stuff," Constancia said, eyeing the papers stacked around the room.

"I've been cleaning out some of my husband's and my files."

"Where is your husband?" Constancia asked, randomly peeking at a box of the yellowed crumbling pages.

Rude, I thought. *This girl has no manners.*

"Today is the third anniversary of his death," she said looking down at Peggy.

"I always cook some of his favorite foods around this time. He liked to eat. It's dumb, I know… I wind up giving away most of it to neighbors." Putting her large hand on her dog's head, she added, "You and I sure do miss him, don't we Peggy?" She went through the arched doors to the kitchen with Peggy in tow, mumbling words we did not ask her to share.

"I'm sorry," Constancia said, looking rightfully embarrassed.

"Me too," I added, feeling an ignition of my own grief creeping up from inside.

"Do you need any help with the food?" Sandra quickly offered.

"No dears, just settle in at the table in the dining room. Won't take me but a few minutes to bake the chicken and heat everything."

The dining room held a great, old, round mahogany table. The four of us sat down, a spectacle with our rough dinosaur-like rashes and protrusions. We chatted as if we were old friends or come together for an evening of sparkling, intimate conversation.

We clicked somehow. I didn't know what to think.

Pearlie brought out nice china, white with a gold and ruby colored trim. I felt cared for and important by this woman's hospitality. Something that had been wound tightly within me began to relax just a little. We dined like queens on roasted chicken and greens, and washed the feast down with soda.

The rain that began when we left Manhattan came down stronger now, heavy and pounding against the gated windows, wind whipping and whistling outside. The sky had darkened to a depressing slate.

Our conversation drifted towards work. "I'm a dance teacher at Roosevelt High School," Sandra shared.

"What losers are over there," Constancia said. I noticed she had pasted a big wad of pink gum on the edge of Pearlie's plate.

"Do you always say exactly what you think, Constancia?" Sandra said cocking her head and smiling gently. Everything about this woman was light and easy, from her delicate bone structure, to the way she held her glass, to her effortless upright posture. Her teeth protruded slightly, but her high cheekbones and clear complexion (no lines, no wrinkles, nothing!) said she had lucked out in the genes department. Well, except for huge glaring rash of scaly ridges on her forehead, of course.

"Of course I do. I'm Puerto Rican." Constancia pointed at herself emphatically.

"I love teaching at Roosevelt. I work with wonderfully talented young people," Sandra continued.

Constancia nodded and then paused with her fork, "I never realized how not smelling things can really affect your taste."

"I'm sorry. I hope that doesn't last for long," Pearlie said.

Only half-listening to the conversation, I busied myself studying Pearlie's house, taking in the magnificent oak bookcases, crowded piles of books, and stacks of framed awards waiting to be given a place of honor on the walls. It all clicked. "I've figured it out—Pearlie, I bet you're a librarian!"

"Yes," she nodded, her smile deepening. "For over thirty years. I worked in just about every borough. Library work gave me everything. I even met my husband when he was the head archivist, for a while, at the Schomberg Center."

"What's that?" I asked.

"*You've* never heard of the Schomberg Center?" Constancia asked with a sneer.

"The easiest way to describe it is that's where they have special collections of texts by black folks. Almost anything you want to know about blacks all over the Diaspora is there. To a librarian, it's a three-story dream," Pearlie responded wistfully.

"God, I know what that is and I ain't even black," Constancia added.

We looked at her. I tightened my leg muscles and breathed in deeply through my nose. My mid-section hurt, as if someone had physically punched me, and I could feel my neck and face flush deep red as I stared down at my lap. A part of me was deeply embarrassed that this gum-smacking idiot knew something, *anything*, that I didn't. I felt, not for the first time in my life, as though I had a scarlet "FB" on my chest. "Failed Blackness." I had heard all the names implied by her comment before from black, brown and white folks. I was an impostor, a traitor, an Oreo. I wanted to lash out at Constancia, I wanted to defend myself, to tell her to shut the hell up, to grab her head and smash it right down on the beautiful blue and white plate in front of her. But, I'm not like her, leaking aggression out of my pores. I'm not someone who seems like a ticking time bomb. I reeled my coil of anger back in and spoke with as much calmness I could muster. "You don't know anything about me, Constancia. You don't know what I like or dislike. You don't know where I've been. And, you don't hold any special secret keys about black people. If you did, you'd be one very wealthy girl."

The small dining room felt claustrophobic right then. Constancia's lips pressed together, her smile faded and she glared at me.

"It's not about being black—anybody could live in the city and not know everything," Pearlie offered a quick smile to me. "It's about living in the city, and knowing its resources and hidden treasures." Pearlie tapped my hand softly, then got up and reached for Sandra and Doris's plates.

"Yeah, whatever," Constancia said. She pulled her trademark piece of gum off the plate and popped it back in her mouth. "You said something about pie? What you got for dessert around here? Maybe I can taste something sugary better than this chicken."

I shook my head, remembering what my mother sometimes said about people. *No home training.*

"I never turn down dessert," Doris quickly interjected, covering Constancia's rudeness. Crazy Doris had been almost as quiet for most of the meal as I had. I wondered what she was making of our gathering. Pearlie came back into the dining room with large slices of pie, setting dishes in front of each of us. "Eat up, now," she ordered.

My still-smoldering anger kept me from registering anything good about the warm slice of pie. It felt lumpy in my throat. *After this, I'm going to politely excuse myself and get the hell out of here*, I thought sullenly.

"And what do you do?" Sandra asked. Oh. She was talking to me.

"I'm an out-of-work ski instructor," I said.

"How'd you get involved in that type of work?" Sandra asked.

"When my father passed away, my mom sent me to live with my uncle in Vermont. My mother could either support us or her art, and she couldn't be bothered to do much of anything else, like applying for aid. My uncle was the only family member on my father's side who didn't mind having a biracial child to raise. My mom had no sisters or brothers."

"Biracial? You don't look half white," Constancia blurted out.

I ignored her. She was being a huge pain in the ass.

"I had been good at track," I continued focusing my attention on Sandra and her affirming face, "I had good legs and I was an angry kind of girl." I shot a quick glance to Constancia, but she seemed oblivious to my warning. "My uncle took me on the slopes and showed me a couple of things. Vermont skiing is real different compared to other places, but I just took to it. I would be out there for hours, or as long as my legs held up. Even though I came to skiing in my teens, it felt like I had been doing it all my life."

A loud crack of thunder made me jump.

Peggy let out a little howl.

"That's enough from you, Peggy. That's odd. No mention of a bad storm for tonight," Pearlie said.

"You must have some dollars to ski," Constancia said playing absentmindedly with her earrings.

"No, I don't actually. I teach skiing, or rather taught skiing, because I loved it."

"So do you have a plan of action to get re-employed?" Pearlie asked. She was now stretched out on an old maroon chaise, with Peggy at her side.

"I'm not sure what I am going to do," I said surprising myself with this honesty. "Skiing instructors get temporarily laid off all the time."

"I think it's wonderful you ski and are trying to make a living from it. If it's your passion you will find your way back to it," Sandra said. The rest of the women in the room—Constancia aside, of course—nodded.

"Is that hail?" Doris said rising out of her seat. She went to the window. We were quiet for several moments listening to pace of the rain pick up. Hail pelted the window and fire escape. *Maybe I won't take off immediately, after all.*

From: Lynx Dupree
To: Dalton Rutland, Director of Operations, KrystàlaVox
Subject: Cultural Competency and Naming of Product #1165
Date: May, 1997

Dear Dalton,

I am bringing to your attention a recent meeting that I had with Heather Johnson, Senior Sales Manager and her team.

I was surprised to learn that my suggested name for product #1165 was not only dismissed but changed in a way that I find offensive to myself and our potential customers.

'Renew You Relaxing Natural Miracle Hair Tonic' was my suggestion. I choose the word renew because it offers up a sense of hope and possibility. This will be the first hair care product released by KrystàlaVox and I thought this name reflects a new beginning.

I also have to admit that in part, I was thinking about my mother who is still in a coma. The name is also an attempt to come to terms with what remains of her legacy in this new company.

I'm a reasonable person and I understand that the sales team gets to make a final decision.

My concern is the reason behind the spelling change. Here is what Grace told me:

"We need something simple and catchy. This spelling speaks to customers in a way that they can understand-you know, ebonics."

Ebonics, really?

I am disturbed by this conversation on many levels. I am offended as an African American. I am offended that Heather and her team have such disregard for the people that may buy this product. As I told her, in marketing black hair care products, there is a history of using word play and clever titling. These, however, were often inside jokes referring to a shared history and knowledge of the communities we served.

KrystàlaVox does not have that thirty-year history that my mother built.

I am deeply troubled by this incident and would appreciate further conversation.

Sincerely,

Lynx Dupree

Senior Research Consultant

SEVEN

KAT

The conversation continued easily through the evening.

I liked talking to them, despite Constancia's frequent asinine remarks. We found Pearlie to be a generous host not only with food, but with her well-stocked bar. I kept the girls up late with stories about skiing, which made us feel cooler—no small feat, given the apartment had no air conditioning. And, with the storm raging outside, we couldn't open the windows, so the apartment was a sweltering trap of humidity and heat. Sandra's hands swelled and the rash above her eye started to weep and ooze, so she had to excuse herself a few times to use Pearlie's bathroom. Pearlie said she needed the one large fan focused on her because of a heart problem, and since she was such a kind host and all, no one questioned her. Not even Constancia. As for me, I didn't mean to talk so much, but I love the sport, so once I get going, it's hard for me to stop. The substance of this conversation felt so different than conversations in Aspen. These women were actually curious about other people. About *me*. When you're giving ski lessons, you're absorbed in making sure people are getting their value and are safe, so conversations hover on the surface. The people I called friends were either couples friends that had drifted away post-breakup with Peter, or other women my age who were looking for a marriage partner, or were most interested in where in the world they would next visit to ski. Most friends were transient: Aspen for a few months or a year, then onward to other peaks. It became easy to show the side of me that pleases all, and reveals nothing.

As the night grew longer, I wondered how long we would be welcome in Pearlie's apartment. It seemed like there came an appropriate time in the evening for us to go and scatter to our homes; the public health department would surely be closed by now. However, nobody got up to go somewhere else. The storm outside raged and we just kept on talking. So, when Pearlie came out with sheets and blankets and gave us sleeping assignments for the master bedroom and the spare room, we all seemed to breathe a collective sigh of relief. I could have taken a cab back home, but for what? An empty apartment haunted by the memory of my mother.

Before retiring, I asked, "Pearlie, can I use your phone?"

"Sure. Use the one in the kitchen."

"Okay, thanks."

I went into the kitchen with its relaxed yellow paint and pictures of her, Peggy, and a kind-looking man with a high forehead, who I assumed was her late husband. The green phone on the wall was old school, with a rotary dial.

I called Ro three times. No answer, just her crisp voice on the answering machine. I absentmindedly stroked the bumps of my rash, which had spread to the back of my neck. Tomorrow, I promised myself, I would go over to her apartment.

EIGHT

CONSTANCIA

Kat has a major a ski pole up her ass. Not even for a second do I believe that homegirl doesn't have no money. No money and she skis? Yeah right, I wasn't born last night.

Tomorrow, I'll call my brother and see if Hector called or came over to the house. These women acted like they didn't have no man in their lives to call or find out about. Hector had pissed me off many times, but I'm starting to cool down from our last argument. I miss him. I gotta work on keeping my anger in check. No more twister, hurricane-strength outbursts.

I don't even know why I'm still at Pearlie's house. It's not the storm keeping me here. I'm just kinda... curious about the women. I didn't ever really hang well with black women before. Well, if truth be told, I don't tend to hang with no one. I mean these ladies were all mostly cool and shit but still... This ain't my style.

Kat, that ski chick, she's interesting to me. Different. I never met a sister like her. I mean, I haven't met a lot of different types of people. My cousins call my family backwards cuz we live in the projects and since my mom died, we've kept to ourselves. Secretly, I kinda wish I could ski. I bet my cousins do. They think they are better than everyone else because they live in Connecticut.

She sounds free when she skis, I wish I could feel free somewhere... sometime. Most of my life has been trying to stay out of trouble's way, trying not to get caught up with shady dudes, fights with other women, making sure I don't get mugged or stabbed walking around my neighborhood. I'm not too worried though because I know how to protect myself. Learned a few things from my brother's friends. Taking care of all that shit though don't leave no time for skiing.

RADIO SHOW: STRAIGHT TALK IN THE COMMUNITY

Brooklyn, August 1998

ALFONSO: Welcome back. If you're just joining us, we're discussing the controversy surrounding the natural hair relaxer Reenu-You and its possible connection to illness in our communities. I'm Alphonso Jones, your host. Joining me, in the studio, are Clifton Jones, commentator and author of numerous books including Will Black People Survive the 21st Century? and Lorraine Simmons, founder of the People's Corner, a nonprofit organization based in Brooklyn. With us by phone is Jazzmin Olsen, health reporter for The New York Post.

CLIFTON: The problem is that the facts the health agencies are telling us changes daily.

JAZZMIN: The Department of Health and the mayor's office are attempting to update the public as things become clearer. They are trying to piece things together.

CLIFTON: Really? Because what I see is intentional confusion. They misled people into thinking that this skin rash caused by Reenu-You was not a problem.

ALFONSO: *Clifton, are you saying doctors ignored this health issue?*

CLIFTON: *Two things. Yes, I think doctors didn't respond quickly enough to take this issue seriously. If several hundred white women came to their doctors with terrible sores on their faces, heaven and hell would have been moved to find out the cause.*

LORRAINE: *I agree with Clifton. I think the slow and botched response speaks to a lack of respect for the health of minority women and lack of health care access.*

CLIFTON: *And, the second thing I want to offer is that this situation is partly about black women, in particular, being obsessed with straight hair. If that wasn't the case, these kind of products wouldn't find such easy targets.*

LORRAINE: *I completely disagree! That is an indefensible statement, Clifton. Don't lay this negligence at the feet of black women. Lots of women—white, black, Latino and Asian— do many different kinds things to change their hair texture, style and color. It doesn't mean you hate yourself if you do. No one expects to buy a defective, frankly harmful product, which is what Reenu-You is.*

CLIFTON: *Lorraine, you know the facts—You can't deny that that there is a long history of hair products damaging black hair.*

LORRAINE: Yes, that's true, but it is also important not to jump to conclusions.

JAZZMIN: If I may interject–

ALFONSO: Please, Jazzmin, go ahead.

JAZZMIN: What we do know is that Reenu-You is a product of KrystàlaVox Company. It's a subsidiary of IvakHealth, a multinational pharmaceutical company. KrystàlaVox acquired the Dupree Corporation a little over two years ago in a hostile takeover. The founder, Jessica Dupree, had a heart attack a few weeks before the takeover and still remains in a coma. The Dupree Corporation was one of the last successful black-owned hair product companies.

CLIFTON: Yeah, black hair products is a multi-billion-dollar business. What was once controlled by smaller black businesses has become the territory of mega corporations like Revlon and Clairol. What do they give back to the community?

JAZZMIN: If I may add one more important detail.

ALFONSO: Please!

JAZZMIN: Jessica's daughter, Lynx, stayed on with the company in their research and development wing. From there, the picture gets a bit murky. The company's research facility is in Malaysia, and reports state that Lynx Dupree went there to develop a new product. Lynx passed away in November of last year, her cause of death undetermined.

LORRAINE: That sounds suspicious.

CLIFTON: Does this mean that this Reenu-You caused outbreak is potentially fatal?

JAZZMIN: We're not sure what she died of. There wasn't an autopsy report. We just don't have enough information to confirm that concern.

LORRAINE: Aren't these products regulated?

ALFONSO: Good question.

JAZZMIN: Well, here is where it gets interesting. Hair product lines have to have EPA approval. All hair products: rinses, shampoos, relaxers can potentially pose a threat to the environment as they are released into drains and sewers and eventually water supplies. Any hair product going has to conform to minimal levels of biological risk and hazard. It seems, and this is unconfirmed, at the moment but it appears the paperwork for Reenu-You was never fully completed, and did not go through the proper channels, but received approval regardless.

ALFONSO: Shocking! How is that possible?

CLIFFTON: *What? So someone in government wasn't doing their damn job. Or, KrystàlaVox paid someone to get around the system? I would bet it is the latter. Troubling!*

ALFONSO: *How many people do we know have been affected? In your community, Lorraine?*

LORRAINE: *We have been hearing complaints for the last several weeks.*

JAZZMIN: *By all accounts that I can gather, there are several hundred women affected.*

ALFONSO: *Any deaths?*

JAZZMIN: *None that we know of linked to Reenu-You.*

ALFONSO: *Our phone lines are open, and we want to hear from you, especially if you've used Reenu-You. After the break, we'll hear from our callers.*

NINE

KAT

I woke up in the middle of the night disoriented. I lay for a few moments watching dark shadows on the wall and smelling foreign smells. I got up, put on my shorts and quietly slipped out the front door and upstairs one flight to the roof. At this point, the storm had quieted to a steady drizzle. The rusty door gave way, unlocked. I'd lucked out. Since childhood, my favorite escapes have been rooftops. When my mom would go into her creative trance where nothing mattered except what she was working on, I would amuse myself on the roof. The air always smelled better up there. Rooftops were a place where I didn't feel like I always had to hold my breath, or prove anything to anyone. It was where I could just be me. That's where I learned about the night, boys, and drugs. I thought, maybe that is the only thing I really missed about New York—the rooftops with all their hiding places and secrets.

A pigeon took off and I heard a voice behind me say, "I beat you here." Out of the shadows, Doris walked toward me draped in a black shawl. I wondered if it had been stuffed in her knitting bag.

"Yes, you did. I didn't mean to interrupt… I couldn't sleep," I said starting to turn away.

"No, don't go. Stay, please." She stood near the door.

I nodded, not wanting to be as rude as I had been before the night of eating and talking downstairs. I looked at her more closely now; her brown eyes looked thoughtful and her whole demeanor was calmer and more contemplative than before. The rash continued to advance across her face, the tail of the spiral stopping above her lips. My mom would have wanted to draw her. I could care less about drawing, but my mother did teach me to notice and pay attention though I could forget to do it.

After a few minutes of silence, I offered, "Why do you think this virus is special?"

"I feel it growing inside me, whatever it is, and it's strong. It's a presence, a life force. It needs us. It's not stupid."

I immediately regretted I had asked her anything.

She kept on in a hushed voice about a "presence," I listened but my mind wandered off to Aspen. I missed my routine of hiking in the morning, three or five skiing lessons in the afternoon, and then my time on the slopes. I missed the weekends, enjoying more of my own time on the mountains. I didn't know what I wanted forever, but nostalgia about rooftops aside, I was damned sure that whatever I wanted wasn't in this hot-ass dirty, cavernous city that had devoured everything I cared about, and had given me this disgusting rash.

"And then when I'm sleeping, it wakes me." Doris continued her ramblings.

I yawned, not even bothering to cover my inattentiveness and boredom.

Doris just kept watching me closely, like she was waiting for something. I stared right back at her, seeing all the crazies of New York reflected in her face. I'm talking about the people who drink their own urine, wear aluminum foil hats huddled in cardboard boxes in alleyways, or think there is a conspiracy behind every crisis… and have mysterious leathery rashes covering their faces that talk to them in their sleep.

"And you know it needs us as a group or unit don't you?" Doris said.

"What?"

"That's why we couldn't stay at the Health Department. Other people were beginning to bother us. It needs the five of us. *Just* the five of us. I think it works better in small groups."

Ok, this lady was fully entering delusional territory. I mumbled something vague about being on the lookout for her observations and left the rooftop in a hurry. Of all the things I could have caught in NYC, of all the people I could have been stuck with, I had to get this hallucinating, delusional weirdo. I should have been glad that I caught this instead of something else. *A virus is a virus is a virus*, I thought. Surely the rash would disappear over time—I hadn't even looked at my face since last night. It might be better now. Or the CDC or the clinic might have a cure for the virus. *It's just a virus.* Even as I thought this, a part of me felt like a marked woman, changed forever.

I awoke the next morning to a scream, followed by wailing. *Constancia*, I thought to myself. I rubbed the sleep out of my eyes, and rushed out into the living room.

"Hector's dead. He's dead. My baby, my baby!" Constancia wailed while doubled over. Yesterday's prominent iridescent green eyeshadow had faded and now just a few green sparkles dotted her eyelids, but her lipstick was smudged red on her chin, her mascara running down her face in black and blue streaks. Her rash looked an angry purple, similar to mine in that it clustered around our hairlines.

Her angular face now possessed a softness and vulnerability that only a grave injury could have coaxed from it. Pearlie held and rocked the young woman. Constancia now wore a scarf wrapped around her head, covering the rash and what was left of her hair; I guess Pearlie had given her one.

Sandra paced with slow, deliberate steps that carried a meditative quality to them. Doris was looking out the window and shaking her head. "Weather's bad again today, too."

"What happened? What's she talking about?" I asked.

"Constancia's received, oh, just awful news, Kat," Sandra's said.

"She called her house this morning..." Pearlie's voice trailed off.

"Last night, he had come back to the house to wait for me! My brother let him sleep there. My brother said this thing, what *we* have was... was all over his body, he was bleeding from his ears, his eyes! He had come over looking for *me*. The police are there now with some doctors. They want to find out where I am. What am I going to do? Oh Dios mío! Oh Dios mío!"

"Honey, you haven't done anything wrong." Pearlie reassured.

Constancia hit her stomach a few times shouting, "Why him? Why is he dead? How could this happen?" Her red-rimmed eyes closed tightly for a moment, then opened wide with shock. her nostrils flared, and her mouth opened and closed seemingly without conscious control.

Pearlie, holding the hysterical Constancia calmly said, "Sandra, will you put on some coffee and get some of the doughnuts in the refrigerator for the girls?" To Constancia she murmured, "You've got to rest for a minute. Lay down in my lap." Obediently, Constancia laid her head in Pearlie's lap turning away from us, allowing her despair to flood into Pearlie.

Sandra gave me a quick glance, nodded and dutifully followed Pearlie's suggestion.

I sat down on the couch and tried to think. Peggy came up to me and pushed my hand with her nose. I rubbed the back of her neck, roughly. Taking this as encouragement she licked my knee.

"Constancia, I'm so sorry. I just don't know what to say," I exhaled sharply.

In a moment Sandra came to the kitchen door holding a box of doughnuts listlessly in her hands. "The virus is mutating. Isn't that what this means?"

"It lives through us," Doris said.

"Will you please be quiet?" I growled.

"There haven't been any other fatalities. There's no reason to think that the virus..." Pearlie trailed off weakly, unable to finish her sentence.

"That we know of," Sandra said.

The rain continued. The house took on a gloomy cast.

Constancia rose up, turning to face us. "Hector's dead! Covered with the same thing I have. That *we* have. Yesterday, he was alive. Can't you see, mamis? We are all going to die."

"Maybe. . . we shouldn't have left." Sandra said.

Even though I was thinking the same thing, I thought better not to say it. "Everybody calm down," I reasoned. "We can go back to the Health Department or another hospital if want. We can go to the emergency room if we need to. Our first concern, however, is Constancia." Though I didn't particularly like her, this new turn of events just felt so awful and surreal I thought that we should get her together so she could at least face her family. That was the only decent thing to do. She didn't strike me as the most stable young woman—this situation might drive her right over the edge.

"He was the only one I had, mi corazón...mi corazón. The only one who ever cared," she moaned, covering her face.

We put Constancia to bed, with Sandra offering to sit watch with her first. Outside, the rain kept coming down. Periodically the strong wind gusts rattled the old windows of the apartment. A dark gray day, promising to get worse. I bit into a stale doughnut and thought about Ro.

Pearlie turned on the television news to see if there was anything useful we could find out, but there was nothing being reported about Reenu-You.

The gloom that had descended upon us after the news of Constancia's boyfriend didn't break until late afternoon. I tried to make grilled cheese and bacon sandwiches for lunch, offering to help as Pearlie looked so tired. I burned two sandwiches because my mind kept returning to Ro. Why hadn't I heard from her? I checked messages on my mother's answering machine and my home phone in Aspen. It was silly to worry, I told myself. She was one of the healthiest people I knew. She hadn't caught any of the childhood diseases (except chickenpox) and in all the years I'd known her, I could count on one hand the times she had been sick. Still, I couldn't shake the feeling something was wrong.

The rest of our group was in the living room talking about the Department of Health. We all knew, I suppose, the right thing to do was to march ourselves to a hospital to be quarantined or *something*. It's hard to say what was keeping us from doing it. It was Saturday and they were closed was the easy reason. But, I guess we all had our reasons. Personally, I harbored deep suspicions about New York City health agencies and hospitals as generally incompetent, but I knew I had decent doctors I could call on back home in Aspen.

In Pearlie's home, it felt like we had escaped to a new emotional territory, a comfort zone in the city. I could feel the ever growing pull to stay, as if my body would resist all other options. It felt familiar. Yet how was that possible? None of us had known each other before yesterday. Here I was cooking—or at least trying to cook—in Pearlie's apartment. I didn't even like cooking in my own apartment. Yet here we were. No one was making a move quite yet. None of us felt sick, though we looked terrible.

Scrounging around in Pearlie's refrigerator, I found two small tomatoes. I chopped those into thin slices and added them to the platter of food I was about to present; grilled cheese and bacon sandwiches, roasted almonds, tomatoes, and Jerkins pickles. "Okay, this is the best I can do on short notice," I said. "I hope you're hungry."

"You've saved the day," Pearlie said clapping her hands. The others made their way to her dining table. Doris went in to the kitchen to retrieve napkins. I called out, "Doris, can you bring my cup of coffee in?"

"Sure," she said. In a minute we assembled and ate.

"Don't you think they'll be calling for us here? Didn't they see us leave with you? You told them we were with you, right?" Sandra asked.

"I did no such thing!" Pearlie exclaimed.

Now I was surprised. "You didn't?"

"I sure don't like the idea of us being poked and pricked," Doris said.

"Oh, now don't you worry about that," Pearlie said. "Not only did I not tell them that we were going to my house, but they have no way to get in touch with me. Those officials don't have my address," Pearlie replied with the first real smile of the day.

We all busted out laughing so hard I had to put down my second cup of coffee. The absurdity of the moment made us fall over. The Department of Health people let us waltz out and Pearlie assisted them with wrong information, so that if they wanted to find us they couldn't. We—a group of five sick, obscenely-rashed brown and black women, with wine and purplish scabs, green-purple scales on our faces, and hair falling out possibly due to an evil chemical relaxer—have temporarily disappeared.

"We've been kidnapped by Pearlie," Sandra said.

"How ironic that a purveyor of records keeps no record of herself," I said.

"The world is filled with mysteries," she winked back at me.

"You don't trust doctors?" Sandra asked incredulous.

"Should I?" Pearlie retorted.

"But, they must have some record of you? Don't you have insurance?" Sandra pressed.

"Oh, I used to trust everyone. I don't think I got wise to anything until my fifties. I gave everything I loved to this city and when my husband got cancer it was like I had worked for nothing. We used to live in Queens in a beautiful little house and all of that. I haven't always lived here, like this." She squeezed her eyes shut for a moment and I wasn't sure if she was trying to snatch back a memory or push one away. We grew quiet.

"We went to so many hospitals and treatment centers, I used to dream of them. I couldn't escape them. Back and forth. I took care of my sister who also died of cancer and a cousin who died of cancer. What did doctors and hospitals offer any of them? Looking at their watches all the goddamn time, explaining nothing and talking down to me and mine like stupid children," she shook her head. "My husband died from a complication from his medications—a medical error, they called it. In the end it wasn't the cancer that got him, it was some doctor who simply wasn't paying attention to what he was supposed to be doing."

"Did you sue?" Doris asked.

"Yeah, I did," she replied. "That's why I'm living in these lovely digs now."

Her voice caught on the last part of her story. I felt a sense of despair and frustration, but not bitterness.

"So, no, whatever *this* is," she continued, "I'm going to find out in my own time. Pray on it. I'm not running to the doctors again. I gave up my old identity. I started living under different aliases. You know how easy it is for a librarian to have access to information?" Pearlie shook her head and laughed. "No, you have no idea. Well, it would make your head spin. I retreated from data sources, passwords, and access codes. To the Department of Health, I am Mrs. Cranbill." Pearlie got up and grabbed a small pillow from the sofa, put it behind her back and adjusted herself.

"Now, I'm not stupid and I'm not a thief. When I got this virus, or whatever this is, I wanted to find out some basic information so I went to the Department of Health. I found you all yesterday and that was good. I haven't had a normal conversation in almost three years. Most of my friends gave up on me. I retreated and started living like a hermit crab, really. There's no excuse for that."

She paused and looked solemnly at each of us around the table. "I'm not telling anyone one here what else to do," she said. "Before I boss people around, I at least like to get to know them at least a few days. But I want you all to know you're welcome to stay a while, or go as you see fit."

All of us were quiet, absorbing her story. Sandra pushed back from the table, stretched, and went over to sit in the rocking chair with her legs pulled up underneath her. Doris had stopped her knitting and stared at Pearlie.

"Is your name really Pearlie," Doris asked, her tone grave.

Pearlie leaned her head back and laughed heartily. "Of course! And, Peggy's is really hers, too."

At the sound of her name, Peggy barked from her resting place underneath the large dining room table. The serious mood broke, we laughed again, and started to eat.

I wondered what my ski friends might think of me now as I sat around a table of women who were so unlike me but whom I liked. I wasn't their token "black friend"—aka a non-threatening black woman, separate from those "other" kinds of black people, who skis and hangs out in Aspen with other (white) Aspen people. I always told those friends that

I despised the city and its inhabitants, that I preferred the conformity of the ski community. I wondered what part of me was talking then. Could it have been the part of me that wanted to run away from my mother? To punish her? She would have relished the hijinks of Pearlie and found some way to paint both her and her dog. My mother always tried to live free without dependence on anyone—not the state, or a man, or even me. Sitting there I felt I could almost hear her whisper to me, "Stay a while longer and find out the rest of Pearlie's and the other women's stories."

The conversation moved on but I gently tried to ask Pearlie more questions about her past and her decisions. She just as gently (and much more deftly) deflected them back at me.

"The past is unimportant. I've got to move forward," she said with finality.

"No, you're wrong, Pearlie. The past makes us who we are," Doris said.

Not being able to figure out how to get Pearlie to open up more, I realized then I was not as good as my mother listening or asking people questions about themselves. Yeah, I could give directions to students on the slopes; that felt natural. When I wasn't teaching, I was usually by myself. I had so much to learn from my mother and now I never would. This self-knowledge saddened and unsettled me.

The conversation through the late afternoon kept going. It was my fault—it started out so casual. I kept telling them how much they would like Aspen, and how beautiful it is in the mornings. And, how Aspen air was a good contrast to the sticky, humid weather of New York. I had my Ford Explorer with me and I kept saying how great it would be if they could see it. Hell, the fresh air alone might do wonders for this virus. Weren't we all going a little crazy not knowing what else to do?

Pearlie finally said, "So are you inviting us or what?"

I swallowed hard, a three-day trip without many stops with four other diseased women. I must be crazy.

"Sure. We're all in this together. After we find out what is wrong with us."

"Even Constancia, if she wants to come?"

"Only if she seriously behaves herself," I said with a look over to Sandra.

It wasn't like we knew each other for our whole lives, but it was an almost intimate familiarity.

"We shall have to leave Pearlie's house sometime. Her generosity won't last forever," Sandra said.

CLASSIFIED MEMO: CIA

July 1998

Agent Jana Ling is on her way to Chicago to investigate reports of a mysterious virus circulating in the minority community. Symptoms of the virus sound similar to experimental work conducted many years ago. Probability of any relationship between the two, however, is statistically low.

TEN

CONSTANCIA

I feel like my whole body is on fire. As if my skin is being rubbed off. I toss and turn. Everything runs together. My whole body is hot. I must have a fever. My thoughts about Hector jumble together. I see us at Coney Island, Rockaway Beach and Great Adventures. He loved rollercoasters. I put my arms up in the air in this dark room. I see his smile when he looked at my designs and how he would go over to the wastebasket and look at the crumpled sketches I threw away in frustration. He would say, "They're good, mami. Stop being so mean with yourself."

How could he be dead?

My thoughts turn evil and dark. Why couldn't it have been my brother or my father?

I will have to face Hector's mother and sister who never really liked me. They thought going to FIT was dumb and that I would wash out. They thought he gave me "too much freedom."

Pearlie keeps coming in and giving me drinks.

How am I going to get up from this bed and move again?

What is there to go back to?
I am lost.

ELEVEN

KAT

Constancia came out later and joined our group, and Pearlie and all of us fussed over her, trying to get her to eat the dinner Pearlie had prepared of salmon cakes, rice pilaf, and broccoli. The vulnerability her face expressed earlier had retreated, replaced by a stony resignation. She picked at her food, still looking like she was in shock. Constancia announced she was going home in the morning.

"Look here," Doris said pushing her plate of unfinished dinner away. "I've been thinking. And you don't believe me when I say that this virus is about something more than cells and DNA and what you can see. It's smart." Doris waved her knitting needle around with her left hand wildly.

Pearlie said, "Woman, will you watch that thing!"

I shook my head, focusing on my breathing. I wanted to scream, *No one wants to be part of your crazy ideas, Doris.*

"How old are you, Pearlie?" Doris asked, unfazed.

"Fifty-nine." We all stared at Pearlie in amazement. She didn't look a day over 50.

"Me and Peggy keep young thanks to Pond's cold cream," she said with a smile and a wink.

"And I'm forty-six years old," Doris said. "Sandra, what's your age?"

She got up and bowed gracefully, "I'm thirty-eight."

"So, what's your point?" I said.

Doris picked up her fork and jabbed the remnant of a salmon cake and popped it into her mouth, "I bet you're in your twenties," she said pointing to me while chewing. "And I bet more than anything, Constancia is in her teens. Don't you see? It needs us... we're all from different eras, different generations, and different timelines. It needs us. We're five different people."

"Of course, we're five different people," Constancia interrupted grumpily with her arms folded, "Anyone can see that."

"I'm twenty-five," I sighed. *A generation is a broadly defined concept*, I thought. "Doris, your argument is more about age than experience," I countered, but I was somewhat taken with the idea.

Her gaze drifted up toward the ceiling, "Yes, yes, I haven't figured out the generation thing—I just know that is a key. I feel it. I don't know that I can figure out the *why*, though. Why does it need the five of us?"

"What is 'it'? And whatever 'it' is, it doesn't need the five of us," I said.

"I bet the other women from the clinic also wanted to get in groups of five," Doris continued, completely ignoring my objection.

"Maybe the virus is not going to kill us, maybe it's going to use us," Sandra offered.

"Use us?" Doris asked raising her eyebrows and leaned in.

"Yes, use us. Like everything else in our life has—used us and thrown us away," Sandra said.

Sandra's comment surprised me; she seemed like the most optimistic person among us.

"Is that how you truly feel? Used and thrown away?" I said.

"It's simple really," Sandra began with her intelligent eyes looking directly at me. "As a dancer, I study the human form, not just bones and muscles, but organs, the circulatory system, the glands, the respiratory system, everything. I have studied everything that helps the human body move and create patterns that we know as dance. In so doing, I have decided that the liver is the best metaphor for women like us."

"The liver, ugh. Why you got to bring that up? That's nasty," Constancia said.

"No, not really. Do you know what the liver does, Constancia?" Sandra continued in her graceful, even tone. "In the body, it plays one of the key roles of taking in and clearing away toxins. Also, when it isn't working properly, it can store strong emotional feelings. Yes, that's right *feelings*," she said, looking at each of us, anticipating our questions before we asked them. "See, we clean up everyone else's stuff in America, we take everyone else's poison and turn it into something useable by the body politic. You name it, we have digested it and made it into something useable. But we are so underappreciated, nothing is ever left over for us. And what we do get back from folks and society is so often negativity. We store all the toxic things in the cells of our body."

"I hate liver," Pearlie replied matter-of-factly.

"My point exactly," Constancia said.

Sandra's words stunned me into silence. I didn't feel underappreciated. What was she talking about?

"Deep thoughts," Doris said. "I've been waiting for a sign from God my whole life."

"I don't know if God can talk through a virus," Pearlie said.

"Oh, and this is God?" Sandra said.

"God has never talked with me. But this virus is a part of God, and because the virus speaks—not, God—to me, it is a conduit for God."

"God forgot about women a long time ago, Doris," Sandra said.

"You are crazy—both of you! Liver and God in all the same breath! You both belong in a fucking loony bin," Constancia spat. With her makeup gone she looked young and tired. She pushed herself away from the table and stomped back into the bedroom. Pearlie got up to check on her. After a few minutes, she walked over to her bar and fixed two whiskey sours. One she carried back with her into the bedroom; the other she left on the coffee table.

I arose from the table and followed to see if Pearlie wanted any help. Inside the bedroom, Constancia hid under the covers, like a young girl. "I can't go back just now. I can't. I've got nothing to go back for. I don't want to see his body. Sandra talking about the goddamn liver. How is that helping me? I don't want to hear that shit."

Leaning in, Pearlie pulled back the covers from over Constancia's head and stroked her cheeks. "You can stay here as long as you want," she whispered to the young girl in a soft voice.

I wondered if Pearlie ever had kids. Or maybe being a librarian prepared you to work with all types of people. I figured she didn't have kids because if she did, they would not have let her live here by herself. Quietly, I backed away from the two women and walked back outside to join the others.

I went back to our circle. Doris continued unfazed by Constancia's outburst. "Okay, what are some of the other things that are special about us? Maybe we can understand why it has chosen us through looking at similarities."

"Maybe we just need to go to the doctor." I said restlessly.

"Then why are you here?" Doris asked. "Why haven't you left yet?"

Caught unaware I stared back at Doris. Why was I still here? The freak storm was one reason, but not a very good one.

"That's just it, right? You don't know, do you? Maybe you feel like you can't leave. Maybe that's the virus keeping you here. Or God," she said, a slight smile spreading across her face.

"I'm leaving tomorrow," I said defiantly. "We're not doctors, you know. We can't figure this out overnight. It doesn't make sense, any of it." My perception kept shifting as if I saw all of us through a kaleidoscope. I felt sorry for Constancia but didn't particularly like her. I bonded with Sandra, but hell, she had all this terrifying anger inside. Pearlie's a loner and been through hell and back. She's like a hip grandmother, and Doris was crazy.

"You hold that thought, Kat. I want to hear Doris's grand theory because it might not prove anything, but it's damn entertaining," Pearlie said returning to the table. "Okay, Doris, lay it out for us. I mean really lay it out for us. We're all ears. Kat, you are going to listen, you hear? Life is a mystery and maybe she is going to help us see a new part of it," she said.

"Thank you, Pearlie, I knew when I first saw you that you were a mystic at heart," she said nodding and conveying an almost unbearable smugness. I had to control myself from rolling my eyes under Pearlie's scrutiny and preoccupied myself with the sink.

"Kat, don't fiddle with the dishes right now. Come on in here."

"Let's make a list," Doris said, a triumphant look on her face.

We identified common points of interest and life experiences. We started with silly, mundane things, like if we used tampons or pads. Later, while crunching barbecue potato chips and sipping on gin and tonics we edged into the territory of lovers, from the intimate to the ordinary. "You did it *where*?" was a common refrain.

"Uh, uh. That can't be a common thread." I said once shaking my head. Sandra's sex list was so long and varied that I'm sure we didn't find out everything about her. She gave me a new perspective on what I might have forward to look forward to in my thirties.

After about four hours, we isolated a few things including the absolute love of chocolate-covered cherries, which probably was not as relevant in comparison to more important things like the fact that all of our mothers had died within the last few years. We were all relatively unattached and with Constancia's age (she groggily called out "nineteen" from the bedroom), we did have a somewhat inter-generational age group. Although I didn't buy Doris's theory one bit, it was, as Pearlie predicted a good way to pass the time.

From: Lynx Dupree
To: Dalton Rutland
Subject: Reenu-You
Date: November 20, 1997

Dear Mr. Rutland,

I write you with the utmost urgency.

Almost a week ago, before I was terminated (unfairly in my opinion), I tested the Reenu-You formula on myself. I would not have taken such a drastic step except that I was so concerned about the acceleration of plans with Reenu-You, without in my opinion full research.

The product does work on the hair as indicated in my initial research—even better than expected.

However, I have felt rather unwell after using it. I have a fever and nausea. I have also noticed a small distinctive strange rash along my left ear. There are other effects that I would rather talk to with someone else about. I urge you to remove Reenu-You from production. I am on my way to see my doctor and look forward to talking with you on my return.

Sincerely,

Lynx Dupree

TWELVE

KAT

After about six gin and tonics each, we were past the comforting moments of reminiscing or energetic upswings of brainstorming our commonalities. The fatigue, stress, and strangeness of the day was wearing all of us down. Constancia joined us; she had stuck to her whiskey sours, but was not as far gone as the rest of us. Hell, she had been sleeping for most of the day.

Sandra sat cross-legged on a pillow near the sofa. Pearlie was stretched out on the couch. I was in a rocking chair.

"Suppose I will not be able to dance... suppose they have to amputate my legs?" Sandra said.

"Oh, you're scaring yourself," I said. The alcohol was kicking in as I had no idea if this terrible rash would start spreading to other parts of our body.

"Maybe you won't be able to ski," Constancia said. "There's no black people that ski anyway. I never see black people skiing on television and damn sure none of *my* people ski." It looked like she was leering at me, but the lights were dim and I was not sober.

Pearlie opened one eye and turned over on the couch and slurred, "Constancia, behave yourself."

Welcome back, Constancia, I thought blearily. In just a few hours she had morphed back to a sullen, annoying young woman. She did not want to talk about Hector; she was not ready to go home. Maybe she wanted to make us pay with all the pain that festered inside. The sympathy I had for her in the morning began evaporating like water poured on a hot griddle.

"What do you want from me? To stop skiing? There's always a *first* someone to do something. I'm not Olympic gold, but I'm damn good and I'm not going to apologize for that. People like you have tried to make me feel guilty for wanting certain things."

"People like who?" She said a malevolent look crossing her face.

"Like you, Constancia! Like playing mind games and attaching a color to everything… I know what inequality is and I'm not trying to limit myself."

Part of me wondered what I was saying to Constancia, what any of it meant, why I could feel a wave of anger crashing against my normally solid defenses. I breathed heavy. I got up too quickly and felt the spins coming on.

Sandra's soft voice said, "Both of you have points, it's just a shame society has made it such that things that are just human are also seen as white."

"Here! Here!" Pearlie shouted.

"I don't need a peacemaker, Sandra. She's got to stop judging everything by its outside cover."

"I don't got to do *nothing*. You don't even know me," Constancia said puffing out her chest.

"Covers are sometimes all that a pair of nineteen year-old's eyes can see," Sandra continued getting up from her seat.

"Why you talking about me like I ain't even in the room," Constancia said turning to Sandra.

"You're acting like you shouldn't be in the room. You're such an angry young woman," I snapped. I felt a part of myself cringe, how many times in the last decade has someone thrown that at me. Still, I was coursing down the slope and the alcohol told me I couldn't turn back now.

"You know, you're not that much older than her?" Doris sang out.

"This isn't funny!" I said.

"It's like Sandra said before, we're not rich and famous chicks. That's why we're sick!" Constancia said.

"Life is more complicated than that. All types of people get sick." I huffed. I had begun to scratch around my neck and hairline. The purplish skin flaked like eczema.

"Oh really, ski bunny? How complicated is it for you?"

Before I could lunge at Constancia, Sandra leapt up and inserted herself between us. "Kat, why don't you go in the bedroom? I'm tired of you two bickering. We've all had way too much to drink to have a civil conversation. We all need some sleep!"

I turned to Doris and shook my half-filled glass of ice and alcohol, "Doris what does that do for your little theory? We can't even get along!"

"We will someday," she said almost dreamily. "This virus has got some purpose for us—we just have to be smart enough to figure it out."

I left wanting to punch Constancia right in the mouth. I went in the bedroom and lay down. My body shook with fatigue, fear, too much alcohol and anger. I had nothing to go home to and no one to call except Ro, and I didn't want to call her again because I was so scared she wouldn't answer because she couldn't.

I found myself awake again late at night. I had a slight headache but nothing that wasn't manageable. Constancia lay passed out on the couch snoring, an empty Mr. Wilson's whiskey bottle on the floor. I assumed that after figuring out she couldn't torment me, she drank some more.

I made up my mind that I really was leaving tomorrow.

Sandra found me in the kitchen rummaging around for something to drink since Pearlie was out of coffee.

"Want to talk about what happened?"

"Constancia's a child," I snorted.

"You got out of a difficult situation and still had your mother's love. Not everybody does," Sandra said in a whisper.

"Is that my fault?" I snapped. My tongue felt furry.

"No, but it makes you accountable."

"No offense, but I sincerely hope this isn't going to be a long sermon on what I owe to inconsiderate girls who come from the projects," I started defensively.

She raised a hand, stopping me from continuing my rant.

"Listen to yourself. I hardly know you, and you *are* a grown woman, but I work with kids, like Constancia. Kids who struggle to find their worth in a world where because of who they are they aren't seen as competent or smart. Maybe your mom gave you love at home—that has nothing to do with color, but not everyone got that love, support or even interest."

I opened my mouth ready to attack again but I stopped and thought for a moment how my mother approved of anything that I did. She was kind, loving and caring. You could be right in the middle of making a mess and she would celebrate it as if it was the best thing she had ever seen. She also sent me away. Was that for the best? My uncle's family did have more to give materially. I did see her often. I had been the one to close her out, she had always been the same: loving, and honest about what she could and couldn't give.

"Aha," I said I grabbing a box of cocoa from back behind an almost empty box of Bisquick and slammed down the box. I poured mugs full of hot water. We sat sipping the tasteless hot chocolate in companionable silence.

"You two want to be alone?" Doris peeked in.

"No," I said shaking my head. "You want some cocoa?"

"Sure," Doris said. "God, I haven't drunk that much since my sister's wedding a few years ago," Doris said, easing herself down into a chair.

"Married?" Sandra looked up.

"Separated," Doris said quickly.

"We're all unattached, it seems," I said. *Another interesting point for the list you made.*

As I got up to make another mug of weak hot chocolate every part of my being registered that the last 48 hours made me feel alive in a way I had never felt before.

There it tapped me again, a feeling of intimacy under all of the hassles, anger, blowups. Despite everything, I had to admit that the last two days were the most interesting I had experienced in a long time.

"Kat, wake up." Constancia urged.

I rubbed my face, surprised I had fallen asleep at the table. Three of us had talked until it was almost daylight and then Pearlie came to join us. I flinched and she withdrew her hand.

"What time is it?" I said

"About six o' clock."

"What do you want?"

"You gotta see this," Constancia said. She motioned for me to follow her into the living room. Stretching, I shook off the night's stiffness and followed Constancia.

Doris, Pearlie and Sandra were all sitting in a row across from the front door. I also noticed there was a small pile of brackish colored vomit to the side of each woman.

"Oh God," Pearlie moaned.

"What's happened?"

"They can't go outside," Constancia said calmly.

"I'm too old for this shit," Pearlie said. With some effort and the help of Doris's shoulder, the older woman rose and took a seat on the couch.

"You got to be joking," I said.

"This is the worst I have felt since we got this thing," Sandra said.

"Pearlie and I were going to go out for food and other things, and then she just started vomiting... see, Kat, I don't know..." Constancia said as she rocked back and forth on her heels, hugging herself.

"Go and get some paper towels and clean up the vomit," I barked. The other women looked incapacitated and I needed a moment to figure out what the hell was going on.

"I just don't believe it," Constancia said.

"Stop saying that. I'll help you, okay, just go and get some cleaning supplies. NOW." My queasy stomach wasn't just because of last night's heavy alcohol indulgence. For a moment, I felt that I might join in the morning purge.

Constancia rolled her eyes at my order, but went into the kitchen.

"I got as far as wanting to open the door," Sandra said.

"It's confining us," Doris said.

I shook my head and I walked up to the ordinary looking buttery colored door. Like most doors in the city it was adorned by a variety of heavy locks and deadbolts on it. The bottom left corner of it housed deep and profuse scratch marks in it, presumably Peggy's handiwork. Taking my time, I unlocked each lock. I felt nothing strange while doing it and the door opened easily. Behind me, I heard a collective sigh of relief.

Constancia stepped between Doris and Sandra and began cleaning up the slick puddles of puke.

I bent down to help her. She brought a trash bag and I held it open as she deposited wet wads of paper towels in it. We worked in silence. Doris and Sandra were still sitting on the floor opposite the door.

"You feel okay?" Doris asked.

"Given everything else, yeah, I'm fine," I replied.

"I guess we're going to the store," Constancia said.

"Looks that way," I replied more tersely than I felt.

I washed my face and threw on my shorts. Unfortunately, Constancia and I were the only ones able to withstand even the *idea* of being outside. Each time Doris or Pearlie opened the door, they'd both start vomiting–either an awful case of the dry heaves or another full-on vomiting round. Sandra got dizzy if she stood for too long. The three of them couldn't stand going out by themselves, it collectively gave them the heebie-jeebies.

Not wanting to continue to clean up vomit for the whole morning, I volunteered to leave. Although I didn't really believe in Doris's whole "the virus makes us one" idea, she seemed to be more and more accurately describing the psychological symptoms of what most of us were going through at any given moment.

Just me and Constancia, what a gift! I thought, as we walked down the stairs. Although the days-long freak storm had finally abated and a crack of sunshine appeared, the sky still looked angry.

I confess to having an ulterior motive for volunteering. Before getting some food and supplies for Pearlie, I wanted to go to my apartment and then Ro's. I didn't tell Constancia until we were outside and on the road.

"We're going to take a slight detour. We're going to take a cab to my house."

She nodded.

"We can go by your place, too" I said. "I can drive you over after I get my truck."

"Not yet."

I played the answering machine when I got back home.

Ro's mother's rich, buttery voice greeted me, "Kat, I hate to impose at a time like this, but I just wanted to know if you've heard from Rogaire... she called me three days ago and said she was really sick, and that she was going to get in touch with you. I haven't heard from her and I keep calling. If I don't hear from you or her tomorrow, I'm driving up from D.C. tomorrow tonight. Call it mother's intuition, but I think something's wrong. Please, call me back."

Shit. "This is bad," I said.

"You and Ro are tight?"

"Best friends. She's my best friend," I said.

"She used the Reenu-You?

I nodded. "We've got to go over to her house," I said. My instincts told me something wasn't right. "Maybe she admitted herself to the hospital or something."

As I searched the kitchen for Ro's spare keys, Constancia picked up a piece of painted fabric, African mud cloth.

"This was your mom's—?"

"Yeah, she started working in textiles before she died." I said, cutting her off.

"I design bags and stuff," she paused.

"I know. I overheard you telling the others yesterday," I said distractedly. Goddamn. *Where are her keys?* I thought.

"Did your mom go to art school?"

"She got into an excellent one and she supported herself for a while but she got pregnant with me and that changed everything. She had me before she could finish."

"Kids are a drag. Do you have any gum?"

"No," I said. "Did your mom think *you* were a drag?" I asked.

"Yeah, she really wanted two boys. Girls were a problem to her."

"I'm sorry," I said.

"Are you sure about the gum? I found some wrappers…" Constancia said.

"No," I said annoyance creeping into my voice. "Never mind." I continued to dig through the drawers, and then—*got 'em*. Holding up the keys, I cried out, "Let's go."

Sitting on my black leather seats and adjusting the rear-view mirror in my truck made everything feel right. My butt missed this truck. I let the comfort of the truck and driving into Manhattan envelop me. I didn't care about the traffic, the women, the virus, nothing. I was back where I belonged.

Being outside the apartment again made me feel more generous for some inexplicable reason. I looked at her and saw—a young girl. A nice face, despite the rash, I thought, even better without the makeup. "Constancia, I'm sorry about your boyfriend. I know I said it before, but I really mean it."

"Everyone at the house has been real nice to me even though I haven't been acting right." We rode for a few moments in silence. "You know any Puerto Ricans?" she asked.

"No, Constancia, not off the top of my head."

"I grew up with a lot of blacks." She turned her head to look out the window.

I nodded. *Good for her*, I thought, not wanting to know what she made of the experience. The streets flew by.

Playing with my plush toy skis hanging on the rear view mirror she said, "I want to get out of the Bronx. I want to see other places." She paused, looking at me. "You've seen other places." she added with finality. "People treat you like shit in New York if you ain't got no money."

"Oh, I could tell you stories about Aspen that would make your toes curl."

Silence.

I looked over at her. Tears flowed down her cheeks.

What else could I say to her? I drove on not knowing how to reach out.

I remembered a face; her face was similar to those girls I had gone to school with but had never quite known. What were their names? Lourdes? Esmeralda? Gladys, Jackie, Frances? These were the people blacks made fun of for wearing colored feathers attached to their hips. The girls poured into two-toned jeans in the eighties, the round ones with heavy blue eyeshadow leaning on a counter. The ones dressing up for Menudo concerts, the ones coming in from a holy roller church on Sundays (usually Pentecostal), the women who staffed the botanicas. I always heard that Puerto Ricans spoke Spanglish, not the *real Spanish*. Had I ever known any of them at all?

She was a scared, obnoxious kid, probably very talented and feeling very trapped. This girl with her attitude and bravado, I thought, could take over the world. But, something sunk inside, because I knew it equally possible that it would be easy for people to overlook her. For all her force and attitude, she'd never be able to take the world by storm. People just won't see her.

She didn't look the part. Neither did I, for that matter. Now with our rashes, would we ever look like ourselves again? I let my fingertips brush the tops of her knees.

We made it past the doorman that I knew without incident and a bit of small talk on my part. The small lobby was tastefully designed in quiet ocean blue tones. I pressed the button for the elevator. I knew my world was only moments from becoming right again. The doors opened and a man with bushy ice white eyebrows shot out and a little pale girl with light blond hair trailed behind him.

"I wasn't finished with the show!" she loudly reported.

"It's done, Christina."

"But I want to see it again! Blue's Clues, Blues Clues and *more* Blue's Clues. I love Blue's Clues!" she shrieked.

We got in and I pressed the 16th floor.

"What a little brat," Constancia said with a sneer. "How long you know this Ro?"

"A long time, I already told you that."

"You'd do anything for her?"

"What kind of question is that?" I shot back. "She's my closest friend."

The elevator climbed interminably to Ro's floor. I started sweating again. The doors opened on the fifth floor and an Asian man stepped on. He wore a black leather collar studded with rhinestones.

"Is this going up? Oh damn?"

"You weren't paying attention, huh?" Constancia said.

"Apparently not," he shot back.

The organizing principle in my life up until this point was to have as much fun as I could possibly muster, skiing and partying. I had not really been given or given myself any other foundation. Ro, though, formed a significant part of my life. She was the connection to my past, buried here in New York. She stayed with me through the horrible periods in my life through prep school, through a brief but scary ecstasy habit, through my one-time fear that I was pregnant. She hadn't abandoned me in all those years even though our lives and interests diverged considerably. I reached for that tendril of being known now more than ever.

I could suffer through the utter randomness of life that brought Constancia, and the rest of the Reenu-You women together, my mother's death, the loss of Peter—all because I knew that once I got off the elevator and saw Ro, my world would right itself again. I imagined myself in that moment like a small, brown and gray homing pigeon being inexorably drawn back home to the roost of friendship.

"That's a dope collar."

"Thanks," the man replied not looking at Constancia.

The elevator stopped on the sixth floor and with the quiet whoosh it took off again.

"Ro? Hey, Ro?"

All her lights were off. I flipped them on exposing an expansive entryway into a dream condo. Her view out of the living room, painted in dark browns and soft gray tones, extended out over Central Park West. An African stool from Zaire stood in the middle of the living room flanked by a sumptuous black setae and black leather sectional.

"Nice crib," Constancia was chewing again. She had found a stray piece of gum on the floor in my mother's bedroom. As it seemed to soothe her I didn't say anything.

In the oversized room, opposite the furniture, hung framed pictures of her with various personalities, several in the hip hop business, oldies like Run DMC, Easy E. and a few unforgettable Jamaican stars like Bujou Banton.

Constancia scanned the wall of several of Ro's former and current clients.

"Hey, that's Run DMC," Constancia said with awe filling in the edges of her voice.

"Yeah," I said noticing how still and quiet the house was. Too quiet.

"She's in public relations."

"She throws parties for these guys?"

"Not parties. She manages people's careers, mostly young guys, gets them seen by the right people. That kind of thing."

"She must know everyone."

"Yeah, just about. She started young."

The only mark in the carpet that showed Ro had once been present was a discarded pair of strappy high black heels strewn across the floor like an afterthought.

"Ro?" I whispered.

I felt my head spinning as the many good moments we shared in this space flooded back to me. Her meteoric rise in her work and my joy in watching her work a room.

Venturing further into the too-quiet apartment, I made my way into the master bedroom. I noted the rumpled emerald satin sheets and a pair of black pants thrown across them ready for the enviable size two Ro to occupy.

Constancia made the only sound in the apartment with her occasional gum pops. Pushing open the door to the master bath revealed no new information. It was one of the nicest features of the overpriced condo with a sunken oversize tub, built-in steam room and beautiful cream-colored tile. Breathing hard, I said to myself, three more rooms to go. Each space a minor victory so far.

"She's probably not here," I said. "Ro is always spending the weekend somewhere at someone's home." I closed the door as we made our way through the long hallway. Three more rooms: an office, a gym and a guest bedroom.

The smell registered first. At that moment I felt lucky I did not have to smell my mother as the cancer took her. I was glad in some ways that she kept me at arms' distance. I'm not that strong, though I put on a good show. I pushed open the door to the guest bedroom and the smell got stronger. A small porcelain bowl held what looked like the remnants of Chinese broccoli, chicken and noodles. My split second guess was that the food had been reheated because the broccoli was the strongest smell. Rotting left over broccoli has one of the most offensive smells known to humankind. And half of a rotting cantaloupe sat beside it. For a moment, I felt I would buckle. No death is here, the picture seemed to say, just foul food.

I was just about to close the door when I saw two ashen brown feet wearing thick blue-black clogs sticking out from behind the black futon. Clogs I gave for her a birthday, a few years ago. I had teased her that I didn't want her going all "crunchy granola" on me. She promised me she wouldn't. I walked around to the side of the bed and just stood and looked.

"Ro, no, oh, please, no!"

My friend lay face up wearing a silk pair of green wide cuffed lounging pants and turquoise cotton T-shirt. In life she was a fair-skinned sister, coloring just shy of baked bread. In death her color had given way to a brackish brown hue on the parts of her body that were still visible. Her physical body was the scaffolding for the thing that had overtaken her. The virus manifested itself with its purple crusts across her body, a soft white fuzz blooming from those hard crusts, reminding me of the fluffy and abstract designs of molding food.

Constancia came up behind me squeezing my shoulder catching me off guard "No, this… this ain't right."

I leaned against the wall for support not taking my eyes off of Ro. My eyes would not close. I could not look away. I went to bend over and crouch down beside my friend. Constancia frantically grabbed my arms and jerked me back.

"Don't touch her! Are you crazy?"

Constancia's slight body, weak, and in that moment easy to ignore, pulled at me. Pushing her away, I kneeled down to look at Ro. Ro's eyes were open, in life they slightly protruded, and now in death they almost floated. Crusts covered the rest of her face and made her unrecognizable. I understood what I was seeing—the virus was absorbing her from the inside out, her own body was breaking down and provided the food for this thing.

"Ro," I said.

"Yo, we need to get out here, no telling what else she was exposed to. This is crazy." Constancia said.

It was my turn to rock back on my heels and wail. I felt like I was going to faint. How could it be possible to see the only other person besides my mother who I truly loved dead? Alone. I was alone, really alone in this world. There was nothing left for me. *Nothing.*

"I'm sorry, Kat, but you got to get up." She pulled gently at my arm. "We gotta go pick up food, and head back to check on the others."

On wobbly legs, I rose and leaned on Constancia's thin frame, momentarily glad to have her there with me. I shook my head, trying to fight the impending disorientation in time and space that spun my mind around and slowed the movement of my limbs. I hoped against hope that somehow it would all turn out to be a horrible dream.

She tugged on my arm. "C'mon."

"Her mother. I've got to call Mrs. Jeneu." I muttered.

"From Pearlie's house, from Pearlie's house." Her voice was soft then and I turned and looked at her. My whole field of vision narrowed to follow Constancia's small pouty mouth. She had not forgotten to put on makeup. I wondered when she had the time to apply it. The outer edges of the lips were traced with a shade of eggplant-colored lipstick and a soft cherry pink filled the inside. A popular style, I found hideously unbecoming. I focused though on her two lips working together. She led me away from the room, from the last of my hopes, the last of my ties to my former life. I could not help but ask myself the question: Is what consumed Ro the same thing infecting Constancia and me?

My mind raced and I could barely keep my shaking hands steady enough to steer my truck. All I could see was Ro's body lying there in her bedroom with the same disease on her that marked me now. Flashes of Ro and my lives tumbled together. Telling her about my first wet kiss by Ramirez in the fifth grade, we at sixteen, in an alleyway, pulling off layers of clothes to reveal outrageously skimpy dresses our mothers would never approve of us wearing to a party, her homemade S'mores oozing with chocolate. I needed to call her mother. I needed to get to a doctor. I needed to get out of New York. I needed a strong drink. I needed for this horror to end.

I drove under the 4 train subway, heading back to Pearlie's place, and had just past the congested traffic of Yankee Stadium at 161st. I barely noticed that the streets were slick with rain. They flew by me as the first hint of night covered the sky. I wondered what my mom would do in this situation. For once in my life, I really needed to talk to someone. Ever since Constancia hustled me out of Ro's house, she remained quiet except for the periodic pop of her gum. Death made itself a visitor in both of our lives in just a matter of days. She had lost Hector, her boyfriend and I had lost Ro, my one and only true friend. Her silence felt unnatural, suffocating even, as if death were creeping closer to us.

I prodded Constancia, "What would your mom do now?"

"My mother's insides got eaten out by cancer," she said and then let out a long sigh. And she then popped her gum.

"Stop snapping that damn gum!" I said, in a flash of frustration. I fought tears ready to spring from my eyes and choked back the wild anger and fear. My throat, raw and swollen felt like it was going to close for good and that I might never speak again. I banged my fist on the dashboard making Constancia jump through I wasn't angry with her. This is something that's going to kill us all, I thought. No. Maybe I'm jumping to conclusions. What were the facts? We had this thing. Hector's dead, Ro is dead and we're still alive. Pearlie, Sandra, Constancia, Doris and I somehow seem to fit together and need each other. Correction, according to Doris, the virus needed us—together. Doris's theory spun around in my head clouding my next logical question—how long does it need to keep *us* alive? When do we die? My mind was doing a poor job at holding together the polarities and sharp-edged contradictions of the last few days.

The rain evolved from a light drizzle to a heavy pour, and the sky darkened, matching my mood. I adjusted the speed of my wipers and for a moment felt comforted by their steady rhythm. Just as I crossed late and quick through a yellow light, a blur darted out in front of the car. It happened so fast I braked quickly, just missing a white and brown mutt that ran out in front of me. Although I could hear my uncle's voice time and time again about not slamming on the breaks like an idiot when going into a skid in rain or ice, I broke too hard and too fast, a death grip on the wheel. In my periphery, I noticed the lights of the stores dotting the streets and it took all of my self-control not to close my eyes as we went into a skid and then did a 180 degree turn. In that one prolonged moment, my eyes bulged cartoon-like, and I felt that strange floaty sensation you get right before you take off in an airplane, or at the top of a rollercoaster. Only my feeling wasn't the excitement of traveling somewhere new or the thrill of coming down a giant hill at break-neck speeds. The moment punched into me the utter inevitability of losing everything—Peter's love, my mother, Ro, my spinning truck. All out of my control. Constancia was screaming, I distantly registered. We skidded and spun some more, until finally, finally my truck stopped.

The swerve left the front of my Ford Explorer diagonally in the right lane while the back was in the left lane—a perfect target for an accident. I grabbed the clutch but before I could reverse gears and recover, the sound of brakes squealing told me I was too late. Everything sped up, from nothing into the instinctual. I reflexively pressed my right arm against Constancia's body even though she wore a seat belt. We both lurched forward when a car hit us. The impact felt sharp and hard, but it wasn't forceful enough to deploy the airbags. We were lucky.

"Oh, shit!" Constancia said.

The engulfing silence came a moment later. "Let me see how bad we've been hit." What has happened to my new beautiful truck? I wondered.

She grabbed my right arm, "Don't get out. Don't leave me," Constancia said.

"What? I have to get out," I tried to reason with her, even though my hands were shaking. "Don't freak out."

With the back of her hand, she wiped away tears and sweat smudging her signature thick black mascara. Placing her hands on the dashboard, she held her arms straight out in front of her, locked. And, she still popped that damn gum. It's a miracle she didn't swallow or choke on it during the accident.

"It'll be all right." I said. *I've got to get away from her for a moment*, I thought. I could feel myself wanting to lash out at her. Everything in me was topsy-turvy. One minute, I felt connected to Constancia and the next minute, I was repelled.

"No, it won't," she said shaking her head and popping her gum even faster. Hunched in her little bolero jacket and swaddled in the scarf from Pearlie's covering her now scabby and balding head, her breath picked up at a rapid pace as if she was about to have a panic attack.

I wanted to scream, "I just lost my best friend. I can't take care of you. I should be the one freaking out!" But I said nothing and tried to focus on the finding out what the damage was to my truck and the car that hit us. A quick glance in my side mirror revealed someone struggling to open the other car's door.

"Maybe you shouldn't get out," Constancia said.

"Can you do something useful and reach behind you for the duffel bag? Please?" I said.

With lips pursed and face tight, she did as I asked.

"See if there's a windbreaker in it," I said.

She rustled around in the bag, pulling out a yellow windbreaker after a few moments of searching.

I turned my attention back to the side view mirror and noticed a big brunette-haired woman standing hands on hips, a deep scowl on her face.

"You could just drive, right?" Constancia asked.

"What the hell is her problem?" I said ignoring Constancia. Why is *she* scowling? Without seeing the damage, I already knew I took the worst of it.

I braced myself and opened the door. When I came around the side and gave a quick glance at my truck, I let out a breath and gratitude flooded my body. I had two big dents, but she had taken the worst of it—her Toyota Camry's bumper hung down, the driver's side of the car sported a mess of wires and crushed metal, and her airbag had deployed.

"Look, I'm really, really sorry," I said as I approached her in the near darkness. "A dog ran in front of the car."

"You saved the damn dog, but look what you did!" she said shaking her head.

The rain's pace picked up again and big cold drops splashed down on us. I wrapped my arms around myself though my thin windbreaker gave me little comfort against the assault.

"Are you OK?" I said.

She took another look at me, scanning me from head to toe. In her hazel eyes, I registered fear and surprise. I thought she might be in shock. The rain plastered her hair flat to either side of her face.

"I'm really sorry," I said again.

The woman tightened her mouth and waited as if for inner confirmation before speaking, "I know you," she said while cradling her left arm with her right hand. I hoped she wasn't in a lot of pain.

"I don't think so," I said shaking my head.

"You're one of the women from the TV," she blurted.

"What are you talking about?" I said.

"From the TV! The infection!" she repeated.

Just as I was about to reply I heard a thumping *Honkkkkk-kkkkkkkk*, making my eardrum feel like it's going to be blown out. I turned to see Constancia in the driver's seat with her hand pressing against my horn as if her life depended on it. I feel a mushroom cloud of a headache bloom over my left eye and I hold my head for a few seconds hoping the nausea would pass. The floating feeling of going into the truck spin reappears inside me for a moment making me wobble.

I heard a car door open and slam. Constancia popped out of the truck and came to stand beside me.

For a moment the woman stood gaped mouth. "You, too! You're both infected with God knows what," she said backing away in terror. Her words hung in the air, condemning us.

Great, I thought, out of all the New Yorkers I have to get hit by the one that is delusional. She, however, looked as if she did know us. But how could that be? Why would we be on the news? Ro was dead and nothing was making any sense. The utter fatigue of the day finally hit me.

"Get in the car," I barked at Constancia.

I gave the woman one last sane piece of advice, "Look, let me take your information. I'm not sure what you're talking about. I think there's been a mistake—"

"I'm going to call the police. You're a health hazard. I shouldn't even be near you. You need to turn yourselves in NOW, before you infect anyone else and the disease spreads," she hissed. She then jogged back to her car and looked as if she dove in under the sagging airbag searching for something.

"Wait, it's not what you think," I began and then stopped. How was I going to explain it to her? *Oh, lady, don't get up-set, we're just women with strange infections who are on the lamb from the public health dept. I look like a spotted circus performer and so does my friend, but we're perfectly harmless.* I probably would have run from us, too, just by the way we looked. I tried to adjust Pearlie's soaked scarf on my head.

"You're not going to do a mother fucking thing," Constancia screamed.

"Constancia, that's not—" I said.

"Shut up! She's looking for her pager or cellphone. Do you want the police to show up? She said she's seen us on TV!"

A car honked and the driver flipped us off interrupting the scene. Cars had been zigzagging the past few minutes to avoid hitting us.

From behind us, I hear "Hey! Hey you! Whatcha looking for? Want to buy sumptum?" We have attracted the attention of a man and woman, across the street, who on first glance, when I stepped out of the truck, I registered as crackheads and had completely ignored. The woman wore a dirty red mini skirt showing off her skinny bruised legs and bare feet. Her companion looked no better wearing an oversize yellow T-shirt, dirty jeans and black sneakers. They were both soaked. Great, I thought, help has arrived.

Before I can register anything else from the couple, I feel air pass me and the next thing I know Constancia is over by the car and has yanked the scared woman by the hair out of her car. Although the woman was bigger, it was Constancia's speed and catching her off guard that made the difference. My rail thin companion deftly wrestled the woman down to the ground.

"Help! Help!" the woman bleated. She struggled and tried to kick Constancia, but Constancia sat on her chest, knees on the woman's arms pinning her to the wet ground. Constancia removed something from her jacket. She pressed a button and a shiny blade appeared, —a very long knife with a black handle; an outlawed switchblade.

"Goddamn bitch! You gonna tell? You gonna tell on us?"

All I can register in this absurd moment is how evenly and methodically Constancia is still popping her gum. Chew, chew, chew, *crack*. And how Constancia's craziness has given our two onlookers probably the best free show of the evening. I had seen switchblades before in movies and television, never in real life, despite growing up in New York. *Does she always carry that*, I wondered, torn between feeling impressed and revolted.

"Oh shit! These some bad bitches!" the man from the street called out. He retreats.

"Constancia! Stop it! I said now trying to pull her off of the woman. I grabbed Constancia's shoulders and pull, but everything coils and tightens and in her superhuman strength moment, I can't budge her.

"Give it to me!" Constancia roars.

The helpless woman drops the cellphone from her hand. "Take it! Take it! Please don't hurt me! I won't say nothing, I swear! I swear!"

This is not happening.

I watch, unable to move, as Constancia tightens her small hand wrapped around the blade. Then, as she gets off the woman, I watch Constancia plunge the knife deep into the woman's upper right shoulder. I hear the mean and sharp sound it makes going through the woman's upper shoulder. With speed and precision, Constancia pulls the knife out.

"No!" I shout, finally able to find my voice.

"Now you have something to scream about," Constancia hissed, backing away and grabbing the woman's large black cellphone before darting back to my truck.

"Oooh, look what she's done," the crack addict woman cackles from across the road.

The injured woman contracts into herself, fetal position tight. Blood streams from her shoulder. She picks herself up and hobbles to her car, locking the door in a wet, bloody scramble. I want to help her but I've also got to get us back to Pearlie's house.

Rushing car lights, snap me back into the urgency of the moment. *We've got to get out of here.* I run back to the truck and speed away, almost running two red lights to do so.

"Gimme the phone!" I yell at Constancia, once we've put a few blocks between us and the scene. Constancia casually tosses it my lap. I pull into an abandoned corner lot that might have once been a gas station, dial 911 to give them an approximate location of where the woman is and then get out of my truck and throw the phone as hard as I can into a pile of trash.

"Why the hell did you do that?" I scream at Constancia, grabbing her roughly by the shoulders. "God, a Puerto Rican with a knife—are you *trying* to be a fucking stereotype?"

"Stereotype! Look that woman was on our ass, and you needed help."

"Help?! Fuck you! I can fucking take care of myself! If that's your idea of help, then boy are you really fucked up! You better hope the ambulance gets there in time before she bleeds out."

"I didn't stab to kill her; it was just her shoulder. She'll be OK," she says casually as if talking about making a turkey sandwich.

I can barely breathe now and can feel the veins at my temples straining. "I'm sure that woman got my license plate down. So did anyone else that happened to be fucking watching! We could fucking go to prison, because of you!"

"She already knew who we were!"

"You don't know that! She could have been delusional! She could have had a concussion!" I said.

"Are you awake? You livin' in dreamland?"

"Shut up," I scream, spittle flying from my lips. "Right now, I am trying to remember that you are actually a human being and not some wild ghetto animal." Constancia retreated into her jacket and curled up into the seat and turned as much away from me as was physically possible. After a few moments of silence, I heard the window slide down. Constancia spit out the wad of gum into oncoming traffic.

At least I would have no gum popping on the ride back to Pearlie's.

THIRTEEN

CONSTANCIA

Shit! I feel like I can't breathe. I've always had a bad temper. My mother warned me someday that it was going to get me in trouble. My father hates that part of me and tried to beat it out of me. Why can't I use my anger for something good? Like people who start marches and stuff. Being out of control mostly hurts me. Though sometimes when I was little, I stood up when I saw someone getting bullied. I didn't mind getting into a fight. But this time right before I got out the car, I felt something else inside me, encouraging me to do something. *Protect, protect, protect!* The word, *protect*, racing through my mind like a pulsating house music beat. Hypnotic. I couldn't resist. Like I had to protect Kat and me. Is that what Doris is talking about when she says the virus talks to her? What the fuck? I didn't hear a smooth, sweet, pretty voice like an angel. I've never had a guardian angel though my mom said everyone was born with two. Mine must be on a vacation right now.

CLASSIFIED CIA MEMO

August 1998

Dr. Rosalind Beecher has briefed CIA agent Jana Ling on the current situation in New York. The "Reenu-You" virus replicates quickly, within three to twenty-one days. Symptoms vary, but begin with a disfiguring rash on the face, neck and arms. Agent Ling speculates that the "Reenu-You" virus is a mutation of the biological agent from our defunct covert bioweapons U.S. facility in Malaysia. The agent may have escaped from the laboratory and been accidently incorporated into the Reenu-You product. Mutations may have caused the virus to evolve from one based on human contact to airborne.

After three years of trials, research was abandoned and destroyed after undesirable and unintentional side effects were discovered in hosts including erratic group behavior. Side effects included loss of individual identity in favor of group identity, group paranoia, and in extremely rare cases signs of possible group telepathy. Tests subjects displaying these side effects were terminated. Agent Ling is concerned with the possible amplification of these side effects in the recently infected. She predicts a high threat to stability of population with possible individuals possessing abilities that are uncontrolled and unstudied.

Dr. Rosalind estimates 85% fatality rate of "Reenu-You" as an airborne virus.

Agent Ling recommends sending a tactical unit to investigate the Malaysian facility.

Agent Ling is working with local officials to minimize risk level and to suppress evidence or knowledge of possible origin of the virus. She has full cooperation to terminate subjects showing any signs of abnormal group abilities.

FOURTEEN

KAT

When we arrived back to Pearlie's house, soaked, angry and tired, we were filled in on what we had missed since we left.

"Oh, Kat, it was awful what they said about us," Sandra began. "That we were intentionally violating a quarantine. They flashed our pictures up there along with some other women. No one at the public health department ever said there was a quarantine, my God. The mayor has been on, too. No one knows what they're doing, they're saying all these things and frankly, they all conflict with each other."

Pearlie handed both of us mugs of tea.

"What quarantine?" Constancia asked. "They didn't say nothing about a quarantine!"

"I know, I know. They are going to quarantine a whole neighborhood in Brooklyn. The NAACP is calling for an investigation saying that calling for a quarantine of some parts of the city and not others is illegal." Sandra said.

"They said they didn't know the skin rash was connected to the virus and that's why there was a lapse in letting the public know," Pearlie added.

"You've got to be kidding me," I said.

Doris shook her head. "It's the truth."

"Constancia tried to tell them," Sandra said.

"Look, Pearlie, I have to get out of here," I said. "I'm getting on the road. I gotta buy myself some time. They're going to trace my truck, and then who knows what else. Ro's dead. I'll decide what to do from the road. I want this whole thing to blow over. Something is not right with all of this. Someone's lying and I'm scared." The feeling of free floating fear came again but I used every muscle in my body to push it back down.

"Did you put down your mother's address when you were at the Department of Health?" Pearlie said.

"Yes," I said.

"Then, you bought yourself some time," she said.

"Well, what about the rest of us?" Sandra said.

"Look, whoever is in is in from here on out. We can make it to Denver in a few days if we sleep in the Explorer and take turns driving." The offer came out of me before I fully considered the weight of it.

Everyone else's gaze slowly drifted over to Constancia, now slumped on the couch, who had been very quiet. I could barely bring myself to look at her, though my hot anger had subsided.

"And you?" Sandra said to Constancia, "Are you in?"

"Yeah, it's my fault we're in this situation in the first place."

I wanted to scream, *no shit! Yes, it's your fucking fault.* But, I said nothing. Constancia straightened up. With shaking hands, she took the black knife out from her pocket and laid it down on the table.

"I just carry this with me for protection. You know where I live. I never used that before to hurt nobody. The woman," she paused, "I don't know. I just got sick looking at her. I snapped, yeah I admit it. I just lost it." Constancia paced back and forth as she talked, "I felt all these things. I wanted to protect you, I wanted to protect me. I shouldn't have hurt her. You don't have to take me, Kat, I know that you don't want to. None of you probably want to."

Pearlie picked up the knife with a tissue and removed it from the table.

Constancia looked like she was going to say something else, but hesitated and flopped down on the couch with her arms wrapped around her head.

I paid attention to the word "protect." When was the last time someone had wanted to protect me, even in the backwards way Constancia went about it? What had awoken in her that wasn't there when I first met her? I stood staring at her thinking of all the dumb things I had ever done in my life and how I was about to do the next dumbest thing. Something inside me said I needed to take Constancia along. It was the same sensation I had been feeling with these women all along over the past few days: part compulsion to be next to each other as dictated by the goddamn Reenu-You virus, but part because I wanted to. I tapped Constancia on the shoulder. "Well, what's done is done. What's over is over." I took a deep breath and smiled at Constancia. The others looked relieved. Frankly, I thought, if this virus made us stay together, how were we going to travel apart? We were stuck with each other. Another polarity moment.

Time sped up. Pearlie packed a few things with Doris helping. Sandra raided the fridge. I sat down opposite Constancia and tried to find the news.

Right before we left, I left a message for Ro's mother saying Ro was dead, infected with the mysterious virus in the city. I let her know I had the virus, too. My voice cracked several times while talking. I told her it wasn't safe to come to the city and no one knew what was happening. I told her I loved her and thanked her for all the ways she had been a mother to me. I don't remember how long I stood there after I hung up holding the receiver. Pearlie gently took it from my hands and hung it up. Wordlessly, she wiped my tears away.

On our final exodus from Pearlie's, we huddled together and walked slow because we were very agitated being outside together. Doris was right again. A mild case of agoraphobia, I think. My silver Ford Explorer, (though dinged on the side yet it still looked better and very conspicuous in Pearlie's neighborhood amongst the old Camaros, beat up Fords, and the "almost-new" Chevys that some guys tended to work on all day), held all of us comfortably.

What had brought me to the city was my mother's death and feeling as if I had lost everything of meaning to me in the city. Yet as I drove out of the city with these women, I felt I had gained a piece of myself.

CITY STRUGGLES THREE WEEKS INTO EPIDEMIC

August 1998

Beauty salons like many places nowadays including restaurants, banks and schools around the city are almost empty of people. People are increasingly afraid of going outside. Still, many are trying to continue to maintain their normal schedules. Missy Ross, thirty-two years old, and Lourdes Navarro, forty-years old keep themselves busy tiding up shelves and restocking items in their co-owned Remedy Hair Spa in Harlem.

Misty's eyes tear up as she talks about the number of her clients who are currently in the hospital. "We're healers in this community. We make women feel good. I hate to think that I helped spread this terrible thing."

This "terrible thing" is the mysterious Reenu-You virus that continues to spread through the city, especially in African American and Latino neighborhoods. Its victims suffer with fever, nausea and disfiguring rashes.

Public health officials have recently issued warnings that "No one should administer or use Reenu-You."

Lourdes says that KrystàlaVox, the company that makes Reenu-You was aggressive in marketing to stylists like her and Missy. "Their salespeople were frankly a little obnoxious. They kept giving us discounted boxes of product. That's not usually how companies operate, but no warning bells went off."

While we talk, Missy dons rubber gloves and gathers all the remaining purple colored Reenu-You bottles from her shelf and disposes of them in a giant garbage bag. Centers for Disease Control staff are scheduled to visit here and other salons, gathering all remaining bottles.

"We gave them a chance because we knew the original founder. I met her at a hair show about 20 years ago. She was so inspiring."

They are talking about Jessica Dupree, a charismatic businesswoman and former head of a powerful and prosperous company. She suffered a heart attack in 1996 and remains unresponsive in a coma.

They feel lucky that they do not have the virus. "We have excellent hygiene here at the spa; we always wear gloves for all our treatments," Lourdes says.

KrystàlaVox has recently issued a tersely worded statement disavowing any intentional wrong doing related to their product. They have accused the deceased Lynx Dupree, their former employee, as someone who could be responsible for corporate sabotage. They have not provided any evidence of this accusation.

"It's a shame because it was a good product and everyone wanted it." Missy adds.

Researchers are rushing to identify a "Patient Zero," a term used to find the first person that may have the virus. "Reenu-You presents us with a lot of challenges," Dr. Page said in a recent press conference. He is leading the team of epidemiologists from the CDC. "We have lost a lot of time with the misdiagnosis of the virus. Finding Patient Zero is like identifying a needle in a haystack now as the product was used simultaneously across many cities and we are still trying to determine the incubation time. We don't have a clear sense of that yet. We think it is anywhere from three days to three months."

An anonymous source working at Columbia Hospital says, "We were frankly caught off guard and our systems have been overwhelmed with the steady flood of cases. For the level of contagion, we currently don't have enough biocontainment rooms across the majority of hospitals."

This source believed that quarantines may be issued to help stop the spread of the virus.

—**Jazzmin Bradford, New York Daily News**

FIFTEEN

KAT

First day on the road

A few of us are becoming immobilized in some serious way. Pearlie is battling an intermittent blindness. Sandra's got extreme cramping in her legs. Besides me, Doris is the only one that can comfortably drive my truck. We talk politics. We talk philosophy, too. I took up knitting when I wasn't driving. It's so hard! I told her I was better at crocheting and she just smiled. I found out that she had gotten her MA in philosophy at City College.

"Philosophy is how you live your life, every single sweaty day of your life. I didn't need no damn degree to tell me that. The day that I realized that fact was the day that I left the program without finishing the Ph.D. Every now and again I've been known to quote a philosopher or two," she said with a wink.

You really *can't* judge a book by its cover. These women keep surprising me.

TRANSCRIPT FROM CITY HALL

NEW YORK, August 1998

ANCHORWOMAN: I am reporting live from City Hall. Behind me, Lorraine Simmons, a community activist and founder of The People's Corner, a nonprofit organization based in Brooklyn. She along with other community leaders has organized a rally here and is speaking in protest of the city's handling of the "Reenu-You" virus. And, yes, I have been encouraged to wear a surgical mask while reporting.

LORRAINE: We have been more than patient in waiting for the mayor's office, the governor's office and public health officials to effectively respond to this crisis. We take issue with the quarantining of mostly African American and Latino communities when everyone is at risk.

[CROWD boos]

Why are we being targeted? We have not seen a quarantine issued in this city since the influenza virus. If you're going to quarantine someone, QUARANTINE everyone! This is OUR HEALTH and we will not let someone hurt us further!

[CROWD Cheers]

We are not stupid. There are currently over 8,0000 people believed to be infected with the Reenu-You virus. It is more women than men and more minorities than whites. Many sick folks are from poor communities. We need on the ground resources. How will we eat, if we are quarantined? How will we work? There are many of us that can't escape to homes in Long Island, Westchester or upstate New York.

Why is the situation here deteriorating so quickly? What aren't they telling us? This should not be happening in the United States of America. Panic is breaking out everywhere, like the virus itself. We, however, need to stay calm, organized and focused.

We demand immediate meetings with the coordinating officials including the CDC and the Mayor's Special Emergency committee. We also call on the Chicago attorney general to open an investigation into the KrystàlaVox Company and IvakHealth, their parent company. And, no, we do not believe that their former employee Lynx Dupree was singlehandedly responsible for the spread of the virus. We want the TRUTH!

[CROWD cheers]

SIXTEEN

KAT

Second day on the road

Peggy made it along with us through Ohio, though she didn't fare well in the cramped space. She was fat, old, ugly, and always smelled like urine, still I was sorry to see her go. We covered her in a blanket, and left her in a field a ways back from the main highway in Indiana.

Just before Constancia got a bad fever she told me that she could see Aspen as I described it… just as white as it could be and she was running around in the snow. Her hair is almost gone now, but she says, "For once in my life, it's goddamn funny I'm not worried about how I look, because I already know that I look shitty and there's nothing that I can do about it." When a tooth came out the other day, she joked, "If my teeth fall out I won't be able to chew gum, which I know will make everyone else happy."

As we make our way across the country, we are careful to avoid others as much as possible. We order food from ubiquitous fast food places, never going in, just using the drive through option. We visit rest stops late at night and don't linger. We drive along backroads and sleep in the Explorer. Every state we make it through, Constancia throws away another bangle, an offering to something, but I don't know for what. She does not share all of her secrets. She keeps saying she doesn't want to be weighed down on this trip. I'm not sure she is going to make it all the way. She doesn't want me to stop though. I think soon though, I'll have to stop and take her to a hospital.

We look crazy and if we get stopped there is sure to be trouble. Who could mistake us? Five dark women with scarves covering our heads, and purple lesions marking our faces. If one of us dies or gets very ill, I guess that blows Doris' theory that we five are necessary. As we travel together, we are noticing that we talk less and can anticipate each other's thoughts more. We are starting to anticipate what we're about to say and finish each other's sentences. Strange.

Reports on the radio state that the virus is mutating the worst for men, not just black or Latino men, but white men, too. The doctors now think, like Constancia guessed, that Reenu-You is the origin of the virus and it mutated rapidly. Now it's an airborne virus, quick and deadly. Small riots are breaking out across city landscapes, like pustules, about the meaning of this virus. Some black leader in Brooklyn is saying it is the greatest genocide trick that he knew of, "They know that black people do their hair with all sorts of homemade and unlicensed products...it's a perfect plot. Someone did this intentionally to us." He says that black women are "chemical prisoners of the hair relaxing industry." The news depresses us, so we take it in small doses.

SEVENTEEN

KAT

Third day on the road

In the end I just wanted to take them out of the city and show them some other life, especially Constancia. In a way they had shown me a part of New York I never knew. Nobody wants to die alone and afraid. We had nobody before, now we have something, and somebody. The virus brought us together. It looks as if I might die a part of a new family, something different, something stronger, perhaps. My mother chose to die at home with loved ones at her choosing. We are always more like our parents than we want to admit. I knew I was going to die; it was just a matter of time.

Who's to say it's going to be such a bad death? Death is about perception, and the ability to focus on a different level of awareness. This is the last lesson I learned from my mother.

We're just driving. I hope that we make Aspen in time to show Constancia.

CNN BREAKING NEWS

September 1998

ANCHORMAN: Several hundred demonstrators showed up at the corporate offices of KrystàlaVox in Chicago, calling for a criminal investigation in the company's role in developing the product Reenu-You and the "Reenu-You" virus. Private security and police officers got into a skirmish and shots were fired. Two protestors were killed and one police officer was wounded.

A state of emergency declaration has been issued in several U.S. cities, including Atlanta, Chicago, Greensboro, Miami, Memphis, Montgomery, and New York.

It is estimated that 150,000 people are infected in the United States alone. Centers for Disease Control director Samuel Hines has gone on record, saying that this virus has the potential to spreading to half a million infections in the next twenty-four to forty-eight hours if drastic measures are not taken.

The Surgeon General, Loretta Connelly has stated that in major cities, "the epidemic is out of control and if we don't get control of it now, we will experience a global outbreak. We need support from the White House to hire a round-the-clock team of spe-

cialists, epidemiologists, and lab and infection experts. We need more people working on this now."

Confirmed deaths linked to the "Reenu-You Virus" stand at 89,005.

The President is scheduled to give a press conference about the outbreak this evening.

THE END

ACKNOWLEDGEMENTS

When you have an idea that takes twenty years to come to fruition, there are a lot of people to thank.

Briefly:

Thanks to the various writing communities that read early drafts of this work including members of the 1996 Clarion Science Fiction and Fantasy Writers' Workshop, the 'Michigan Writing Group' and the 'Writing Women' of North Carolina (Linda, Robin, Nancy, and Ashley). Your insightful comments nurtured the ideas in this manuscript.

Thanks to writing teachers: Maureen McHugh, Gregory Frost and Marjorie Hudson. Thanks for being there when I needed you most.

Thanks to recent beta readers: Sarah Tucker Jenkins, Val Nieman and Quanie Miller.

Thanks to my sister, Melissa: thank you for your continued belief in my ability to tell stories.

Thanks to my partner, Timothy. Thank you for being the most patient, encouraging, loving and kind person that I have known on the writing journey, and in life!

Thanks to Ana and Thea and the Book Smugglers Team. I am so grateful for your support and enthusiasm for giving this novella an opportunity to live and play in the world.

.

ABOUT THE AUTHOR

At the age of six, Michele's mother turned a walk-in closet into creative space just for her daughter. That closet became a portal and gateway to self-expression. Michele pretended that Will Robinson, a character on the television show Lost in Space was her brother and that she fought alongside Lindsay Wagner who played The Bionic Woman. And, she went on many other adventures. From that age on, Michele never doubted the power of the imagination.

Her main love is writing science fiction though she also is known to write poetry and creative nonfiction, too.

Her work has appeared, or is forthcoming in *100wordstory*, *Glint*, *Thing* Magazine, *Flying South*, *Oracle: Fine Arts Review*, *Carolina Woman*, *Ms.*, *The Feminist Wire*, *Western North Carolina Woman*, and various anthologies. Michele was a "My View" monthly columnist for *The Chapel Hill News* from 2012-2014. Her award winning blog, The Practice of Creativity, was featured in *Southern Writers* Magazine.

She is currently at work finishing a short story collection.

Michele is completely undone by the sight of pugs and has to restrain herself from collecting any item they appear on. She lives in Pittsboro, North Carolina with her partner Tim. Come visit her at The Practice of Creativity (micheleberger.wordpress.com).

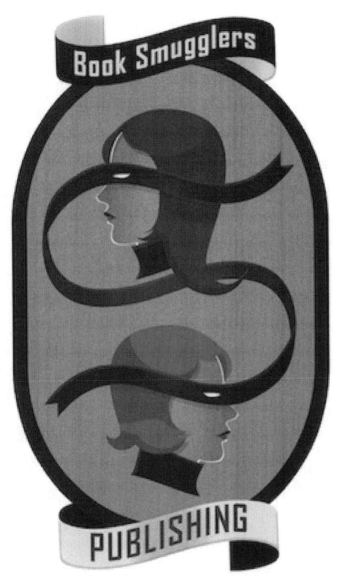

Visit www.booksmugglerspub.com for upcoming short stories, novels, and other publications

74975972R00087

Made in the USA
Columbia, SC
13 August 2017